PRAIRIE SCHOOL

Other Books by Lois Lenski

Autobiographical

A LITTLE GIRL OF NINETEEN HUNDRED

Historical

PHEBE FAIRCHILD, HER BOOK
A-GOING TO THE WESTWARD
BOUND GIRL OF COBBLE HILL
OCEAN-BORN MARY
INDIAN CAPTIVE
BLUEBERRY CORNERS
PURITAN ADVENTURE

Regional

BAYOU SUZETTE
STRAWBERRY GIRL
BLUE RIDGE BILLY
JUDY'S JOURNEY
BOOM TOWN BOY
COTTON IN MY SACK
TEXAS TOMBOY
PRAIRIE SCHOOL
MAMA HATTIE'S GIRL
CORN FARM BOY
SAN FRANCISCO BOY
FLOOD FRIDAY
HOUSEBOAT GIRL
COAL CAMP GIRL

For
my prairie children,
with love

PRAIRIE SCHOOL

by

LOIS LENSKI

J. B. Lippincott Company

PHILADELPHIA ⋎ NEW YORK

COPYRIGHT, 1951, BY LOIS LENSKI

PRINTED IN THE UNITED STATES OF AMERICA

Tenth Printing

Library of Congress catalog card number 51-11169

CONTENTS

Foreword

A letter from South Dakota reached me in May 1948. My book, Strawberry Girl *had found its way into a tiny one-room rural school just west of the Missouri river, near the North Dakota state line. The pupils wrote to tell me how much they had liked the book, and what a difficult time they had to find others I had written.*

"When there was snow, and the cold winds blew," the teacher wrote, "we gathered in a circle around the register and the children listened with rapt attention and speculated on the outcome." Little did I dream, as I read those words, that one day I would visit that school and tell its story.

During the winter 1948-1949, which I spent in Florida, I read about the terrible snowstorms on the Great Plains, and the dramatic rescues by private airplanes and U. S. Army bulldozers. As I read, I kept thinking about that little school, the teacher and children there. I wondered how they had managed to live through those storms. But I could not write to inquire. I had not taken their letters to Florida, and could not remember the teacher's name or their postoffice address.

In February 1949, another letter came.

"The children are having a tough time," the teacher wrote, "but they never complain. Since the severe blizzard the first week in January, they have had to walk as much as two or three miles, since no horse, car or truck can get through the drifts. Today it is twenty-five below. We are having school in the kitchen of the teacherage and it is crowded, but they are cheerful about it. We are finding out what an old time winter is like."

*For the rest of that winter, and all through 1949-1950, a winter de-
scribed locally as "worse than 1948-1949," vivid letters from teacher
and pupils came to me, describing their rigorous and dramatic life. I
knew now that theirs was a story that needed to be told—the modern
instead of the old-fashioned blizzard, when man's mechanical devices
of which he is so proud, fail before the fury of the elements.*

*I planned to go to South Dakota in April 1950, but reports of a late
spring, bad roads and continued snow deterred me. I went in May,
and was marooned for a week in the small hotel in the town, by a
blizzard on May fifth. Here I wrote the first draft of five chapters—
my first experience of actually writing a story on location, in the region.
When I was finally able to go out in the country, nine miles to the
school, I made the trip, appropriately enough, in a skidding jeep during a blinding snowstorm!*

*During my stay, I saw and felt and sketched the real prairie for the
first time. I slept on a cot in the back of the schoolroom—one night
entirely alone in the building—and I learned to feel quite at home
there. I ate my meals with the teacher in the teacherage, and shared
the children's lunches. All the children's dramatic experiences at school,
in their homes, coming to school and going home, became real to me,
as I witnessed their setting, and as I came to know the children themselves.*

*This is no synthetic, manufactured adventure. Their story, as I have
told it, is the essence of truth. It is an under-statement—I feel keenly
my own inability to do it justice. Many important facts, incidents, side-
lights, etc., have had to be omitted.*

*"They never complain—they are cheerful about it," writes their
teacher. Of such solid stuff is childhood made. And their teacher too.
I hope that this book gives high honor to the prairie children. And I
hope that it pays a well-deserved tribute to the heroic rural teachers of the
Great Plains, in South Dakota and the surrounding prairie states.*

To Ruth Carter and the children of Maple Leaf School, McLaughlin, South Dakota, go my most sincere and grateful thanks. This is their story, not mine. Without their help, this book could not have been written. Not all the incidents used happened to them in person. In many ways, the story is a composite, for the sake of enrichment. Names and incidents have been chosen from the region, and will be recognized as authentic by those who live the prairie life.

This "prairie school" is closed now. The building stands deserted and neglected, as the cold winds whistle through. But the prairie children are, and always will be, very much alive.

Lois Lenski

McLaughlin, South Dakota, May 1950

Greenacres
Harwinton, Connecticut
August 30, 1950

The song Born of the Wind, Song of the Prairie Children, *with words written by Lois Lenski and music by Clyde Robert Bulla may be freely used or mimeographed by any schools or teachers interested in its use for children. Its reprinting for any commercial use is, however, forbidden by copyright. It is hoped that the song will be an incentive to the making of dramatizations of the story.*

Born of the Wind

SONG OF THE PRAIRIE CHILDREN

WORDS BY LOIS LENSKI

MUSIC BY CLYDE ROBERT BULLA

CHAPTER I

First Day of School

"She hasn't come yet."

A boy and a girl on a small spotted horse came galloping up to the prairie schoolhouse. They slid off and turned the horse loose.

"No, she's not here," said the girl. "We're in plenty of time."

The schoolhouse looked shabby and deserted. The front porch was sagging and weeds grew high in the yard.

"Look, Delores!" said her brother. "Somebody's broken a window."

"Konrad Snider did that last year, don't you remember?" said

1

the girl. "His ball landed on Miss Martin's desk."

The two children had blue eyes and straw-colored hair. Their cheeks were rosy from their ride over the South Dakota prairie. They were dressed in faded checked shirts and blue jeans. The boy was half a head taller than the girl.

"Look at these steps," said Darrell. "Broken down again. I'll have to bring hammer and nails and fix them, I suppose."

"Wish we could go to that nice new brick school in town," said Delores. "I'd like to ride on a bus."

"You'd end up frozen stiff in a snowbank," said her brother. "They can't run busses so far out. There's our town—Oak Leaf!"

He pointed to the north, where the tiny Oak Leaf depot stood beside the railroad track. Just beyond rose a tall grain elevator. Off to the right stood a single house, empty and deserted. On the other side of the tracks a grass fire was burning, sending up dark, smoldering smoke.

"Some town!" laughed Delores.

"First they called it Kukuk," said Darrell. "Mrs. Kukuk was Russian and named the postoffice after herself. Then somebody changed the name to Tuttle, and that got changed to Oak Leaf— I don't see any oak trees around anywhere."

"Oak Leaf had sixty people once," said Delores, "but they all moved away. I guess it was too windy for them, or too snowy in winter, or too far out. Papa said there used to be two stores, a lumber yard and lots of houses. I wonder what became of the houses."

"They moved one or two into town," said Darrell, "and the wind blew the others down. So everybody moved away."

"Even the Swartz's have gone," said Delores. She looked across the prairie to the deserted house. "Poor little house—it looks lonesome."

"It'll soon have company," laughed Darrell. "The field mice and prairie chickens and skunks will soon be moving in. What's that—a jackrabbit?"

"Looks more like a dog," said Delores. "He's coming this way."

"It's Spike. The Swartz's Spike," cried the boy. "Here, Spike! Here, Spike! Come here, old boy."

The dog, a large shaggy shepherd, came bounding up.

"Do you suppose they forgot him?" Darrell patted the dog to make him stop jumping. "They moved to town last spring. I wonder if he's been here alone all summer."

"He acts like it," said Delores.

"He's so glad to see us. He must be hungry," said Darrell.

"I wish Miss Martin would come," said Delores. "She'll bring food and give us something to feed him."

They walked back to the teacherage door.

"Wonder why she's so late," said Delores. "She ought to be getting here. The first day of school is tomorrow. Look, Darrell, is the grass fire getting worse?"

The children looked across to the field beyond the railroad track, where a cloud of smoke was rising. Now and then it lifted and showed leaping flames beneath.

"The wind's not in this direction," said the boy, "so there's no danger. The prairie grass always burns off every year."

"Let's ride over to the track and watch it," said Delores.

They called Sugar and mounted, then rode quickly over, with the dog Spike following. The fire was licking its way along the railroad embankment, leaving a charred stretch of black behind it. Darrell pulled up the horse in front of the depot, and they watched the fire in silence.

"Good thing Pop plowed that fireguard," said Darrell. "Two furrows along the fence—that'll stop it."

"It won't jump the track, will it?" asked Delores.

"I told you the wind's in the other direction."

"I hear a car." Delores turned and looked. "Teacher's coming."

Over the brow of the rolling hill beyond the schoolhouse, a car was crawling on the winding prairie road, coming closer and closer.

"That must be Miss Martin," said Darrell. "Nobody else would be coming this way today."

They raced Sugar back to the schoolhouse and dismounted just as the dust-covered car drove up.

"Hello, hello!" called Miss Martin, smiling. "Glad to see you." Miss Martin was small, thin and wiry. She was dressed in a new checked suit and wore a red hat with a gay feather. Her eyes were bright and sparkling. "How nice to have a welcome—and some help with my unloading. But what's the matter? You both look so serious. Aren't you glad school opens tomorrow?"

"We came to tell you . . ." began Delores. She stood on the teacherage steps and looked over to the elevator and depot.

"There's a pretty bad prairie fire, Miss Martin," said Darrell.

"You think I'm afraid, don't you?" Miss Martin smiled.

"Mama said if you are afraid, you're to come home with us and sleep at our house," said Delores.

"It has burned off three sections," said Darrell. "Down by our place the men burned a backfire to make it come this way. They're still fighting it with sacks and water over on the other side."

"Yes, I saw it from the road," said Miss Martin. "I wonder how it started."

"Pop says he bet somebody's been burning tumbleweeds," said Darrell. "Summer's been so dry, there's an extra big crop."

"You mean Russian thistles?" asked Miss Martin.

"Yes," said Darrell. "When they get dry, they break off at the stem and roll along like a ball. The wind sends them tumbling across the prairie until they pile up against somebody's fence. Some people don't want their fences broke down by tumbleweeds, so they set fire to them. Then the prairie grass starts burning too."

"It sure is windy today," said Delores. "It's a bad day for prairie fires—the grass is so dry. That fire might come awful close."

"The Bauers over in the brakes had to move," said Darrell. "They were burned out—lost everything."

"Oh, I'm sorry to hear that," said Miss Martin. "They are Peter's and Hulda's grandparents, aren't they?"

She opened the door of her car and stepped out. Spike came running up, panting.

"Why, whose dog is this?" asked Miss Martin. "Yours?"

"It's Spike, the Swartz's dog," said Darrell.

"Oh yes, I see it is," said Miss Martin. "It's good to see Spike again. He's always friendly." She began to walk around the building. "It hasn't changed much," she said. "Still the same broken steps, the same broken window—and weeds right up to my door. I'll have to clear a path to get in."

The children helped her pull tall ragweeds up by the roots. Then she went up the teacherage steps, took a key out of her purse and unlocked the door.

"Let's go inside," she said. Delores followed.

"I'll unload your car, Miss Martin," said Darrell.

The teacherage was a name given to two small rooms at the back of the building, where the teacher lived. The door led into a small square kitchen. The furniture was simple—a table, cupboard, chair and two stoves. One was a two-burner kerosene stove for cooking and the other a coal heater marked *Heatola*.

Delores looked up at the ceiling and smiled. "How do you like your smokehouse, Miss Martin?"

The shadow of a frown passed over the teacher's face. "It hasn't been painted!" she exclaimed. She went into the bedroom. "Oh dear! No bureau. I'll have to get used to living out of cartons and egg crates again."

Delores did not know what to say.

"At least I have my own bed," Miss Martin went on. "That makes it homelike. It won't take me long to get settled."

Delores looked at the bed. It was a cheap metal cot with sagging

springs. The mattress was thin. "If you come to our house," she said, "I'll sleep on the davenport tonight, and you can have my bed. It's wide and comfortable, and it's got two featherbeds on it."

But Miss Martin was not listening. Back in the kitchen, she opened the door into the schoolroom. Six wide windows faced the east, and let in the only light. A large desk stood in front, two bookcases and a piano in corners. The children's desks were arranged in three rows. Blackboards lined three sides of the room. Two doors led into the front hall, which served as a cloak room.

"It's not painted!" cried Miss Martin, looking up at the high ceiling. "Oh, they promised to paint it, didn't they, Delores? Don't you remember—at the picnic on the last day of school in May?"

"I guess so," said Delores, ashamed.

"If the fathers would help, it wouldn't be such a big job."

Delores remembered that her mother had offered to paint Teacher's kitchen herself. Mama always had a paint brush in her hand. She was always painting something. But she had never found time to paint the teacherage kitchen.

"Mama's so busy . . ." Delores began.

"I'll have to sweep and dust before I can move in." Miss Martin went into the front hall and down the steep cellar stairs. Delores went with her, and they looked in the coal bin. "A little coal left over from last winter," said Miss Martin. "Maybe we won't need so much this year."

"Papa says it's gonna be a soft winter," said Delores.

They came up the stairs again and went outside. Darrell had unloaded boxes and cartons of books, brooms, mops and dustpans, groceries and suitcases, and piled them in a pile at the teacherage steps.

"Won't you come and sleep at our house tonight, Miss Martin?" asked Delores anxiously.

Miss Martin looked across the prairie again. The billowing smoke seemed to be coming closer. "Put the things back in the car, Darrell," she said.

"You'll come home with us then?" asked Delores.

"No, it's quite safe to stay here," said Miss Martin. She added, almost in a whisper, "I must get used to it again." Then aloud: "I'll only take in one suitcase and a box of groceries." She pointed to them. "And the kerosene can and the five gallon can of water. I'll leave everything else in the car for tonight."

"Got anything to feed Spike?" asked Darrell.

"Spike? He'd better go home," said Miss Martin.

"The Swartzes left Spike here when they moved to town last

June," said Delores. "Didn't you know that?"

"They've moved to town?" Miss Martin glanced at the deserted house. "I thought the house looked empty. Now I'll have no neighbors at all." She paused. "Here are some sandwiches left over from my lunch. Give them to Spike."

Darrell loaded everything back in the car again. Then he brought Sugar around and climbed on her back. "Come along, Delores," he said. "We got to be gettin' on home. I got all the chores to do."

"Darrell, I'm not going," said Delores. "I'm going to stay with Teacher tonight. Mama said if she wouldn't come, I was to stay and sleep by her—this first night."

Darrell sniffed. "A lot of protection you'll be. You'll put out the prairie fire, I suppose, when it starts to burn the schoolhouse up."

Miss Martin laughed. She put her arm around the girl's shoul-

der. "But I'm not afraid, you know. Why, I've lived in a teacher-age for so many years . . ."

"Don't you ever get lonesome—all by yourself?" asked Delores.

"Lonesome?" Miss Martin laughed gaily. "I haven't time." She went in the bedroom, took off her hat and suit, and slipped on a cotton dress. "Let's get the brooms and sweep."

Darrell rode off and the sound of Sugar's hoofbeats died away. Miss Martin opened the windows, and she and Delores swept and mopped until they were tired. The light faded and the high-ceilinged schoolroom grew dark. Miss Martin filled the kerosene lamp and lighted it. She opened a can of baked beans and another of apple sauce. She and Delores sat down and ate.

To Delores, it was a strange meal. Teacher ate such funny things. She never baked *kuga* (cakes) or made *casenipfla* (cheese buttons) like Mama did. She just opened cans and warmed things up. She never fixed big dishes heaped high with mashed potatoes; she never made big bowls of brown gravy. She never ate *wuerst* (sausage) at all. No wonder she was so thin.

"I must get some bedding," said Miss Martin, after supper. But she did not go to her car. She stood silently on the back porch for a long time. Delores came and stood beside her.

The prairie stretched so endlessly off in the distance. It was not "flat as a pancake" as people so often described it. It was rolling. It rolled and tumbled like the great waves of a mighty sea. There were no trees at all—how homesick a person could get for a tree! And yet there was a grandeur and a majesty about this barren landscape. The brown velour texture of the grassy prairie slopes was beautiful. Miss Martin took Delores' hand in her own. Delores was a child of the prairie. She had never known any other life.

The woman and girl felt very small in the immensity of sky and land before them.

Miss Martin spoke softly: "Sometimes last year, early in the mornings, I used to see a mysterious house far away to the northwest, across the prairie. It was shining so white and beautiful . . . I wished I could go there . . ."

Delores laughed. "It wasn't a house, it was a mirage. There's no house in that direction. Sometimes when I'm riding I see a beautiful town, with high walls and towers. Mama laughs and says it's foolishness. Then, an hour later, it's only the slope of a prairie hill."

"Yes, I know," said Miss Martin. "I always wish I had time to stand and watch the mirage fade away . . ."

"Are you afraid of the prairie fire, Miss Martin?" asked Delores.

"No, Delores," came the ready reply. "If it comes closer, we can get in the car and ride to your house . . . even in the middle of the night."

Night at the schoolhouse seemed very long. It was August and the air was hot and close. Delores wished she had gone home with Darrell after all. She could not sleep. The teacherage felt so strange, not cozy like home at all. She was lonesome for Mama and her little brother Christy. She could smell the smoke from the burning prairie grass and felt sure it was coming closer. She listened to Miss Martin's regular breathing. Then all at once, she heard footsteps. Somebody was walking around the school building with heavy treads. Should she wake Miss Martin up?

Who could be out there on the prairie, nine miles from town? There was no one at the depot or the elevator at night, and the Swartzes had moved into town. Maybe it was the dog Spike. If they fed Spike, he would stay at the school now. Spike was a good watch-dog. He would take care of the school.

Then she smelled smoke again. The fire must have jumped the track. Maybe it was moving toward the schoolhouse. Delores heard the footsteps again—*ka-lump, ka-lump, ka-lump.* She burst into tears and Miss Martin woke up.

"What's the matter, Delores?"

"I heard something . . ." the girl began. "Look!" she pointed to the window, where a dark form could be seen.

"Who is it?" called Miss Martin, rising in bed in alarm.

But the intruder did not answer.

"WHO IS IT? GO AWAY!" said Miss Martin in a loud voice. She put her hand on the girl's arm. "Don't be afraid, Delores."

The figure did not move. Heavy footbeats could again be heard. The figure nuzzled against the window frame and gave a little snort.

"Oh, my goodness!" cried Miss Martin, laughing. "It's a horse. Delores, look. A horse is poking its head in our window. Good thing the window is so high off the ground—he might have walked in."

Delores had to laugh. Miss Martin got up and the startled horse went trotting away. She looked out at the teacherage door. "Horses!" she cried. "There's a whole herd of them. They've come over here because of the grass fire. But it's all died down now."

"I'm glad of that," said Delores. She looked out the bedroom window and could see it still smoldering along the tracks, and knew the danger was over. She fell asleep quickly, and before she knew it, morning had come. After breakfast, she helped Miss

Martin unload her car. Over by the elevator, she saw the herd of horses, eating grain, and recognized them as her father's.

"Eight o'clock," said Miss Martin. "The children will soon be here."

The Sticklemeyers came first. There were six of them—Jacob, Fernetta, Sophie and Wilmer, one in each grade from the third through the sixth, besides the twins, Donna and Bertha, starting in the first grade. They drove up in their cart, a homemade box mounted on two wheels, pulled by their twenty-year-old horse, Buckskin. They all jumped out and Jacob took the horse to the school barn and unhitched the horse.

Miss Martin was kept busy greeting everybody. Konrad Snider and Emil Holzhauer each came on horseback. Ruby Englehart came riding behind her father on his big white horse, Silver. Ruby was eight and had blonde curls. She was pretty and knew it. Last of all, the little Hummels, Peter, seven, and Hulda, six, came in panting from walking two miles and a half across the prairie.

"Is everybody here?" called Miss Martin at the front door. "What are Konrad and Wilmer chasing?"

"It's a goose," said Sophie Sticklemeyer. "The Swartz's goose."

"They left their goose here," said Delores. "They left Spike, too."

"Here comes the Galloping Goose!" shouted Wilmer Sticklemeyer. The goose came up on the porch and the boys tried to chase it in. But Miss Martin stood in the doorway. "Is everybody here? Let's go in."

"Everybody but Darrell," said Delores.

There was so much to tell Miss Martin, it was hard to settle down at first.

"Miss Martin," began Ruby Englehart, "my little sister Mamie fell in the water tank one day in the hot summer. She was throwing boards in and nearly got drownded."

"Oh no!" said Miss Martin. "How did she get out?"

"My little brother Matt said, 'Mamie you better get out,' and Mamie got out," Ruby went on. "My Mama found her standing by the tank all dripping wet. She got a blanket and covered her up. She almost got pneumonia, but the doctor gave her a pencil . . ."

"A pencil?" The other children laughed.

"Do you mean penicillin, Ruby?" asked Miss Martin.

Ruby nodded. "One shot and she got well quick."

"I fell down out of our haymow," bragged little Hulda Hummel. "I was doing the morning chores . . ."

"You? The morning chores?" Miss Martin looked down into the six-year-old's face. Long dark bangs hung into her eyes, and her face had a serious look. She was getting old before she was young.

"Sure, we get up at four o'clock and do the chores," broke in Hulda's brother, Peter. "If Hulda hada hit the stanchion, she'da been killed."

"By golly, that's nothin'," said Jacob Sticklemeyer. "I fell in our dam once . . ."

Delores Wagner could not keep still. "Me and Darrell fell off Sugar and Mama nearly had a fit . . ."

"I went rattlesnake-hunting up on Thunder Butte," said Emil Holzhauer, "and I killed ten rattlesnakes." Emil was thirteen, the oldest boy in school this year. The little children looked at him wide-eyed, and full of respect.

Only Ruby could match the rattlesnakes. "I nearly got froze to death in a snowbank last winter . . ."

"There! There!" laughed Miss Martin. "I know that prairie life is full of many perils, but let's not exaggerate."

"*Exaggerate?* What's that?" asked Emil.

"Make it sound worse than it was," snapped Delores. "Don't be so dumb. If you don't know a word, go look it up in the dictionary."

"But I *did* kill ten rattlesnakes," insisted Emil.

"And I *did* fall in our dam," said Jacob.

"And I did fall down from the haymow," said little Hulda. "I hit the cement floor so hard, for a long time I had to hold my arm out to keep my side from hurting."

"She never told Mama a thing about it," said Peter.

"Well, we are all still alive and we are here safe and sound, to begin a new school year," said Miss Martin. "Will you choose your seats?"

A mad scramble followed, with a few pushes and shoves, before they all got located.

"Where is Darrell, Delores?" asked Miss Martin. "Isn't he coming?"

"Maybe he didn't get home with the cows," answered Delores. "They graze about five or six miles from our place. Or maybe he has to work today. Harvest isn't over and Pop's short of help. Papa thought there wouldn't be no crop at all. First we had hail, then drouth, then it rained and brought the green lice and the grasshoppers. But they've got to harvest what's left."

"There goes Darrell now," said Jacob Sticklemeyer. "He just thinks he's smart. He's showin' off."

The noisy hum of a motor drew all the children to the windows.

They saw Darrell driving his father's tractor down the prairie road. It pulled a wagon load of wheat. The tractor skirted the schoolhouse on its way to the elevator. Darrell lifted his arm and waved, grinning, as the children called to him.

"Can Darrell drive a *tractor?*" asked Miss Martin, astonished. "He's only eleven."

"He was twelve in July, Miss Martin," said Delores proudly. "Papa made him wait till he was ten before he'd let him drive it, but he knew how long before that."

"My cousin drove my uncle's tractor when he was seven," said Konrad.

"Darrell's just showin' off," said Jacob Sticklemeyer. "That's why he hauls wheat past the schoolhouse on the first day of school. I can drive a tractor too, but Pa makes me come to school."

Miss Martin thought of all the days of school Darrell would have to miss during the year. She sighed, but said nothing.

The children settled into their seats again.

"Delores, will you pass out the books?" said Miss Martin.

Another school year had begun.

CHAPTER II

The Fair

"Mama, there's a wagonload of Indians out there," said Delores. She came running in the kitchen door of the Wagner farmhouse. It was Monday, Labor Day, a week later. "They're going to the Fair, too. It's Charlie Spotted Bear and his family."

"Now what do *they* want?" asked Mrs. Wagner.

"He wants some money for the land Papa leases from him, and Papa won't give him any. He told him he paid the rent for this year to the Indian Agency at Fort Yates, and he might not want Charlie's land again next year."

Mama Wagner shook her head. She was a plump, good-natured, soft-hearted woman. "Here, take this bread out and give it to them. Get the eggs from the chicken coop for them too."

Delores brought the eggs and bread to the wagon, where two Indian women and several small children were waiting. They smiled and accepted the gifts gratefully. Then Charlie Spotted Bear climbed up on the wagon seat, and the two skinny horses started off.

"Have they gone?" called Mama from the back door. "Let us go then if we are going."

"Darrell, hurry up, you old slowpoke!" shouted Delores.

Darrell drove the farm truck up to the back door. Mama climbed into the cab and Delores lifted three-year-old Christy up to her lap. Then she climbed in herself. The boys, Darrell and Philip, his older brother, and Emil Holzhauer, who had come over the night before, jumped up in the back. Papa Wagner slipped into the front seat, started the engine and drove off.

Bouncing up and down over the prairie road they went, making three or four turns, until they reached the highway. The country looked brown and barren in the fall of the year. The prairie grass had been cut and stacked in large haystacks in the hayfields, for winter feed for the cattle. Most of the wheat and small grains had been harvested, leaving fields covered with short dry stubble. On the highway, called the Yellowstone Trail, the Wagner truck was only one of a stream of trucks, cars and Indian wagons drawn by horses, making their way to town for the annual Fair.

"Papa," begged Delores, "can I have some money to spend?"

"I want candy," cried little Christy. "Buy me candy bar."

"Money, ach!" snorted Johannes Wagner. "Always money the

kids are asking for. What you do with money?"

"Ride on the merry-go-round, buy some ice cream and some Rooshian peanuts," said Delores. "You gave Darrell fifty cents and Philip a dollar."

"I pay the boys for their work," said Johannes.

"You make them work too hard," said Mama. "They are yet too young—Darrell only twelve and Philip but fifteen."

"Too hard, nothing," said Johannes. "What are boys for, but to help their father? At ten, I was working like a man to help my father on that first claim of his west of town. I never got to go to school except when there was no work to do at home. I never had no money to spend."

"I want candy," cried Christy. "Buy me candy bar."

"Those were the hard times," said Mama. "Grandma Wagner, she keeps on telling us how hard it was in 1909, when this Dakota country was opened up, and they let white people settle on the Standing Rock Indian Reservation. It took her a long time to get used to it, but now she is no longer homesick for the old country. She likes it in town, where she can see her friends and have her kitchen in the latest style."

"And all her eight children and thirty grandchildren to come and visit her," added Johannes, chuckling.

"Will we go to Grandma Wagner's?" asked Delores.

"We go first to Lavina's," said Mama, "to see how she gets along with her two little boys. Then to Grandma's, but if her head hurts, we not stay but a minute."

The truck crossed the railroad tracks and came into the town, which lay sprawled out on a flat plateau, surrounded by flat-topped buttes and rugged hills. It was a shabby, dusty town, unsheltered from the glare of the hot September sun. At its edge stood a lofty black water tower, on which the town's name was painted in white letters. Beyond were two tall aluminum grain elevators, shining like silver; at their feet, dozens of cylindrical grain bins filled to overflowing with recently harvested grain. Several great mountains of wheat were piled near by on the ground.

"Ach! Such a waste!" growled Johannes Wagner. "All the good wheat lying loose on the ground, when so many people in the world go hungry."

"Why is it so, Johannes?" asked Mama.

"Bad management," said her husband. "I read in the paper, they have not enough freight cars. So they let the good wheat lie and rot. After all our hard work to get a good crop."

They drove down the main street, which was crowded with cars, trucks and people. A carnival was set up at a crossing.

"There's the merry-go-round," said Delores. "I wonder, will Teacher and the other kids come?"

"Do not stop, Johannes. First we go to Lavina's," said Mama firmly.

"I get down here," called Emil Holzhauer from the back.

Papa pulled up. "I go with Emil," said Philip.

"Darrell, you stay by us," said Papa. "You go see your Grandma first today."

"Oh, shoot!" said Darrell. "Always you make me act the baby."

A few minutes later, the Wagners pulled up beside a blue trailer-house on a side street, where the oldest daughter, Lavina, now married to Melvin Nagel, made her home.

"Such a house for the cold winters!" cried Mama. "It makes me think of the sod-house I lived in when I was a girl, out by

Hettinger. Then, there was no brick, no wood, nothing to build our house out of but prairie sod. But now, with hundreds of dollars to spend, they buy such a shack on wheels. Not so good as a sod-house, not so warm."

"But it *is* warm," insisted Delores. "They've got bottled gas. Lavina don't like to live in the country and Melvin can ride the tractor out to his farm every day."

"Yah—twenty eight miles out," said Papa, shaking his head. "Almost to Mobridge and back every day. In town is no place to bring up two big strong boys. They should have three or four hundred acres to run on and farm work to do. Boys in town do nothing but loaf and get in trouble."

The door of the trailer-house opened, and there stood Lavina, with a fat baby boy on each arm, twins a year old. Lavina was plump and smiling. "Come in, come in, everybody," she said. "Make yourself at home."

Mama and Papa and the children went in. Papa complained: "No place to put my hat. No place to put my big feet. If I turn around, I bust some dishes. Such a place to live."

"Now, Papa, you just stop it!" said Lavina sharply. "I'm tired of that kind of talk from you. Where I live is my business, not yours."

Darrell and Delores sat on the narrow couch, which opened up at night for a bed. Mama stirred some soup that was cooking on the tiny electric stove. Lavina put her babies on the big bed in the farther room, and Christy climbed up to play with them. Everybody visited for a few minutes. Then Darrell said: "We gonna stay here all day? I thought we came to the Fair."

Papa Wagner reached in his pocket and tossed a half-dollar to Delores. "You two—run over and see the Grandma first."

They hurried out. Grandma Wagner's little white frame house sat on the next corner, with a yard neatly fenced around it. Inside, the lawn looked dry and brown, and several trees were having a hard time to grow. As the children came up, Grandpa Wagner came out the back door. He had a white mustache and walked very straight.

"Hi, Grandpa!" called the children. "You goin' to the rodeo?"

"No," said Grandpa. "I go take a walk. I go to the store to buy groceries."

The children ran in the house, calling, "Your head hurt, Grandma, no? You feel good today?"

"Ach! Look who iss here!" cried Grandma Wagner. "How you haf scared me!" She threw her arms around her grandchildren and hugged them. She was a tiny little woman, no bigger than eleven-year-old Delores. But her blue eyes flashed, and though she had recently been ill, she hopped about with the lightness of a bird.

"What you making, Grandma?" asked Delores, sniffing.

"Prune *kuga*." Grandma winked. "I make prune coffee cakes, six big ones."

"When will they be ready to eat, Grandma?" asked Darrell, rubbing his stomach.

"Just before you go home tonight," laughed the old lady.

"What you been doing, Grandma?" asked Delores. "Painting the house again? Making crepe-paper flowers? Embroidery? Crocheting?"

"I show you. Come with me," said Grandma. "Your shoes clean?" She looked at their feet and shook her head. *"Nein, nein.* Get that rag and wipe the dust off. Then I let you walk on my carpet."

After their shoes were carefully dusted in the entry, Grandma

led the children into the front room, where the shades were pulled
and everything looked dark and mysterious. Crocheted tidies covered chair backs and arms, artificial flower bouquets stood on
small stands and the window sills. A sign on the wall, printed in
shiny red, blue and gold, said: "How Beautiful Heaven Must Be."

Grandma pointed to the what-not in the corner. "See!" She
stood back proudly. The children stared at a new bunch of artificial flowers in a blue glass vase.

"What are they made out of?" asked Darrell. "That's not
crepe paper. What kind of fuzz is it? Cowhair?"

"Ach, you dumb-bell!" scolded Delores. "Cowhair nothing."
She turned to Grandma and asked softly. "Is it velvet?"

"*Nein,* not velvet," said Grandma. "*Chenille* it iss called. I
learned it from Mrs. Musser, who had it from Mrs. Hunstad, who
had it from a lady in Pierre. I send off by mail to buy the chenille
in the bright colors."

"They are BEAU-TI-FUL!" said Delores. "They are more beautiful than real flowers."

"Real flowers—they wilt and die," said Grandma, "but these
never. When first I came to America, to this dry prairie country
where the flowers do not grow, I thought I should die. My heart,
it was sore, it broke in two. I cry all the time, day and night. I
plant the flower seed, they come up, they wilt and die. Never
to have flowers to bloom, and to make bouquet in the house—
what kind of country is this we come to?"

Delores put her arm around her grandmother's waist. "Now
you have pretty flowers," she said.

"That will never wilt and die," added Grandma.

"Aw, heck! Who wants flowers anyhow?" cried Darrell. "I

thought we came to the Fair. The rodeo will be over."

"Run along, children," said Grandma Wagner. "Come back tonight for the prune *kuga*."

Dutifully, they kissed her good-by and ran swiftly down the street.

The Fair Grounds was close at hand, on the west edge of town. Cars were parked on all sides, and the grandstand was nearly filled with farmers, townspeople, ranchmen and Indians. The band was blaring noisy music.

"Jeepers! We're late," said Darrell. "Hurry *up*."

Delores thought she had never seen so many Indians before. They had come in from Fort Yates to the north, and from the Indian towns on the Grand River to the south. There were old wrinkled Sioux Indian men, fat women and young squaws carrying babies wrapped in gaily colored blankets, and leading little children by the hand. Their wagons stood beside their smoky tents in the field adjoining the Fair Grounds, while their horses were hobbled near by to graze. There they built smoky campfires, cooked their food in big kettles, and lived during the three-day holiday.

"Hi, kids! Where you goin'?"

It was Uncle Gustaf, their favorite uncle, who had a hardware store in town. He pulled Delores' curls, jerked Darrell's hat off his head and pulled his shirttail out. He found seats for them at the top of the grandstand. The performance was half over. A calf-roping contest was going on.

"Oh look!" cried Darrell. "There comes Fritz—Emil Holzhauer's brother. Boy, how he can ride. Just watch him."

The calf was turned out of the chute first, and then the rider.

Fritz galloped madly across the arena after the calf, roped and threw it to the ground. His horse kept the rope tight so the calf couldn't get away, as Fritz tried to tie the calf up in so many seconds. Then it was hauled off, and another calf came in. The crowd was excited and hilarious, giving each rider a noisy welcome.

Uncle Gustaf bought the children orange pop to drink and Russian peanuts to chew.

"Don't know why they call them peanuts," said Delores. "They're nothing but sunflower seeds, roasted and salted. Grandma said the only kind of flower that would grow in the West River country was sunflowers. She used to roast the seeds in a kettle herself—then chew them."

"Your Grandma and grandpa learned to chew them in Odessa," said Uncle Gustaf. "When they went from Germany to live in Russia, in the days of the old Czar, to show the Russians how to be good farmers, they learned to chew sunflower seeds there. They called them 'the popcorn of the Ukraine.'"

"I don't care what they called them," said Darrell, "I call 'em Rooshian peanuts." He put a few in his mouth and began to chew, spitting the hulls out at one side.

'I'm glad Grandpa and Grandma came to America," said Delores. "Instead of being Germans or Russians, we're Americans. Miss Martin told us that in America, people come from every country in the world."

"If your grandparents had stayed over there," said Uncle Gustaf soberly, "your Pop and your uncles would have been killed in the wars a long time ago. You might not even be here."

"Oh, look at those crazy cattle!" cried Darrell.

Brahma bull riding had begun. The cumbersome but powerful

animals were hard to stick with, and their riders were having a difficult time.

"Look at their funny drooping ears, and the big humps on their backs," said Delores. "They don't look like cattle at all."

"Remind me of the buffaloes that used to range all over the Great Plains," said Uncle Gustaf, laughing. "But when I go hunting, don't let me meet one."

The people cheered wildly, as one event followed another. The afternoon wore on until the sun began to descend in the west. Then suddenly, the rodeo was over, and the people made their way back to main street and the carnival and cafés in town.

"Got to leave you kids now," said Uncle Gustaf. "Might be some customers waiting at my store. Don't want to lose any trade." He hurried off.

"Oh, there's Miss Martin and Ruby and the Sticklemeyers," said Delores. She ran over to join them, while Darrell slipped off in the crowd to look for Philip and Emil.

"Why, here's Delores!" said Miss Martin.

"Where have you been?" asked Fernetta Sticklemeyer. "We looked for you everywhere and thought you never came." Fernetta and the younger children had their mouths full, stuffed with candy.

"Let's take a ride on the merry-go-round," said Miss Martin. She bought tickets, and they all climbed on, and went round and round to the music. Then Miss Martin took them all to Jen's Café where they had hot-dogs, pop and ice cream. The little children poured their pop over the ice cream and said it tasted good. It was getting dark when they came out, and heard the beating of drums.

"We must see the Indian dance," said Miss Martin. "We're

just in time—before the crowd gets too thick."

At the main intersection the Indians were dancing in the street, circling around the flag pole. The Indian women had started the squaw dance. They wore long graceful costumes, capes and shawls decorated with beads, fringes, tiny mirrors and animal teeth. The monotonous chant began and they started around the circle with shuffling step. The setting sun shot rays of brilliant red across the western sky, as the crowds gathered and watched.

The squaws stepped aside. The beating of the tom-toms began again, and the braves came forward by ones and twos. Their costumes were of skin, decorated with bells, shiny mirrors, cattle horns and turkey feathers. The crouched figures moved with up-bended knees. The music grew wilder and the figures moved faster, until they seemed in a frenzy of movement. Then the music as suddenly stopped. The dance was over.

The watching children caught their breath in surprise. For a few moments they had been carried into another way of life, a way of life lived long ago. Then the illusion was broken. They were back again, standing in their own familiar Main Street. The moments of magic were gone.

"Don't they look silly," giggled Ruby Englehart, "when they dance?"

"Silly?" answered Delores. "That's the way they've always done it."

"Since long before the white men came," added Miss Martin. "It's about all we've let them keep of their rightful heritage."

"Just the same," Ruby went on, "I wouldn't like to be an Indian and live in a log hut down on the river bottom."

"If you had been born there," said Miss Martin, "you would like it as much as they do."

"But I wasn't!" answered Ruby. "My Daddy's a good farmer."

"Does he own his farm?" asked Delores.

"No, he leases it from the Indians," said Ruby.

"So do all our fathers," said Delores.

"All the farms around here are on Reservation land," said Miss Martin. "We owe a great deal to the Indians."

"Here comes old Eddie Good Dog, selling bows and arrows," said Delores. "I wonder who buys them."

The crippled old Indian passed by, mumbling to himself. A group of white boys followed at his heels, teasing and poking sticks. The old man turned and tried to catch them, then went on his way again.

"There's Ma and Pa," cried the Sticklemeyer twins. Fernetta gathered her brood together, and said good-by. Ruby went to join her parents at the Café. Delores was left alone with Miss Martin.

"Can we take you home to the teacherage?" she asked. "I'll ride in the back of the truck with the boys, and there'll be room for you in front."

"Thank you, Delores," said Miss Martin. "I have to leave my car at Schweitzer's garage for a few days." She turned uncertainly.

Just then a young man, whom Delores had never seen before, stepped up and touched his cap politely. He had a brown weathered face and friendly brown eyes.

"All ready to take off, Miss Martin?" he asked.

Delores stared. Did Miss Martin have a boy friend that nobody knew about? She had always said she was too old to get married. Nobody knew her exact age, but Delores insisted she looked young. She had only a few gray hairs.

"This is Paul Kruger, Delores," said Miss Martin. "Don't look so worried. He won't run off with me."

"Who *is* he?" asked Delores. "I never saw *him* before."

"He's one of my boys," answered Miss Martin, "one of the first pupils I had in Twin Butte School fifteen years ago. Little did I realize then that Paul would fly the Hump fifty times in the war. He's had plenty of experience. He's going to *fly* me home."

Delores' mouth dropped open in surprise. "You gonna *fly*?"

"Don't you be frightened, Delores," said her teacher. "I'm not. I'll be home in the teacherage before your father gets his truck started. Good-by." Miss Martin and Paul Kruger walked off and left the astonished girl standing on the street corner.

"Good- . . . by . . ." stammered Delores.

She turned and ran as hard as she could go back up the street to Grandma Wagner's house. The house sat on a slight rise at the south end of town, overlooking a wide stretch of open prairie. Delores stood for a minute and looked north. Down by the Fair Grounds she heard a roaring that faded into a softer humming. Then she saw an airplane lift its wings from the ground, go soaring overhead like a huge butterfly, and disappear in the sun-streaked evening sky.

"Jeepers!" she said aloud.

She felt suddenly hungry. It was a long time since the last hot-dog. She turned to go in.

"Grandma's prune *kuga* will be ready to eat," she said to herself.

CHAPTER III

The First Snow

"Oh look! Here comes the real Galloping Goose!" shouted Peter.

It was a mild day in the middle of November, and the children were playing ball in front of the schoolhouse.

"The train! The train!" they shouted, forgetting their game.

The daily passing of the train was always an event in their lives. The engine pulled a combination passenger-baggage car and a caboose. It had been nicknamed the "Galloping Goose"—no one knew why. The branch line railroad ran across the state line into

North Dakota, and was used for hauling freight, baggage, mail, express, and sometimes passengers.

"That's a new Diesel engine," said Darrell, pointing to its striped front. "I like it better than that smoky, pokey old steam engine."

"Bet she can't pull so good," said Emil Holzhauer.

"Bet she can pull ten times as good," said Darrell. "We'll count the freights when she comes back down from North Dakota tomorrow and see."

"Bet she can't pull through the snowdrifts in winter," said Emil.

"Look! The Goose is stopping at Oak Leaf depot," said Delores.

"Getting ready to haul those grain cars full of wheat back down to town tomorrow," said Darrell.

"There's *our* Galloping Goose."

Hulda Hummel pointed to the pet goose, which came waddling up on the porch. The children took bread from their lunch pails and fed it. It waddled slowly off again with a proud air, as if it owned the whole prairie.

At the morning recess, Delores came running in.

"Look, Miss Martin," she cried. "It's snowing already. When Papa saw how gray the sky was this morning, he said, 'It looks like snow,' and Mama told him he was talking through his hat. But maybe he was right."

"It's been such a nice fall," said Miss Martin. "It can't be snow— yet."

But it was. The snow came down gently at first, as if testing out its welcome. To the children, the first snow was always an exciting thing. The rigors of the previous winter forgotten, they thought only of the wonder and novelty of the falling white flakes. They ran and danced in it, they held up their hands and tried to catch it, they let the wind blow it into their upturned faces. Even after they came indoors, they could not forget it.

"See the big snowflakes!" cried little Donna Sticklemeyer, pressing her nose against the window pane.

"Biggest snowflakes in all the Dakotas," bragged her sister Sophie.

"Man alive! Are we getting the snow!" shouted Konrad Snider, rushing in.

"Huh! That's nothing!" scoffed Emil. "Ground's not even white. Wait till the drifts cover up the windows and you can't see out."

"That'll be something, sure enough." Darrell Wagner shook his head and frowned a little, remembering. He turned to Miss Martin, who was helping him with his Arithmetic. "I don't like to think about it."

"Nor do I," said Miss Martin softly. "It's beautiful—but it makes so much extra work for us all."

"Extra work!" cried Delores. "You said it."

The children were more interested in the snow than in their lessons. They kept lifting their eyes from their books to the falling flakes and the darkening sky.

"It's getting colder," said Wilmer Sticklemeyer. "I hear the wind blowing."

"I must put more coal on the furnace," said Miss Martin.

She went down cellar and the children could hear the dull thuds of her hatchet against the great lumps of bituminous coal. They could hear the sound of shoveling, followed by the sharp bang of the furnace door.

Jacob Sticklemeyer threw an arrowhead across the room, trying to hit Emil Holzhauer on the head. But it hit his desk instead, and bounced over on the large open register in the center of the floor, and with a sharp clang, went down out of sight. Jacob jumped down on his knees to see where it went. As he did so, he got his face full of the soft coal fumes rising from the furnace. The children giggled. He jumped back to his seat just as Miss Martin appeared, panting.

"Delores, please light the kitchen stove, to warm up the lunches," she said. "Baked beans again today?"

"No'm," smiled Delores. "Stew this time."

From the front hall she brought a quart glass jar, tightly packed with meat, potatoes, cabbage, beans, and other vegetables cooked in a thick gravy. "Mama said to put water with it and warm it up good."

"We brought sauerkraut and potatoes," giggled Fernetta Stickle-meyer.

"Would everybody like hot cocoa today?" asked Miss Martin.

The children cried eagerly, "Yes, yes!" "Yah, yah!"

"Hulda, would you like to wash the raisins?"

The children laughed. Washing the raisins was little Hulda's big job. She wouldn't let any one else do it. She emptied Miss Martin's raisins into a bowl, covered them with water, and washed them between her hands. She set the bowl on the register, to let them get soft. Then she dipped them out of the water and carefully placed them in a glass dish.

A history lesson was still going on. Suddenly a loud whisper came from the kitchen door. *"Stew's ready. Want me to turn the stove out?"*

Miss Martin shook her head. "Sauerkraut and cocoa," she whispered back.

Soon the classes were dismissed for lunch, and a bustle of lunch activity began. The children ran back and forth from schoolroom to kitchen.

"We haven't got much today—only bread and cookies," said Peter Hummel. He and Hulda looked into their half-gallon pail.

"I'll give you some of our stew," said Delores.

"I ain't hungry," said little Hulda.

"Ma always sends too much sauerkraut," scolded Fernetta Sticklemeyer. "If we take any of it back home again, she'll give us heck.— Somebody's got to help us eat it." Fernetta spooned out large helpings on china saucers for her brothers and sisters and for the two Hummel children.

"Want any sauerkraut, Ruby?" asked Fernetta.

"Not on your life." Ruby turned up her nose. "I wouldn't eat anything that smells as bad as that. I've got *wuerst*."

The children laughed.

"She means sausage," explained Delores. "The Dutch will come out."

The children settled down at their desks and, hunched over, began to eat. Solemnly little Hulda passed the raisins around, then set the glass dish on Teacher's desk. Delores brought cups and poured hot cocoa out. She passed the cocoa around.

"Yah, I see, Delores all the time gives Emil Holzhauer that big white enamel cup," said Fernetta Sticklemeyer.

"Well, he's the biggest," said Delores. "He ought to get the most."

"And me—you give me the worst cup of all," complained Ruby. "It's cracked and got a chip out. My cocoa's cold too."

Nobody paid any attention to Ruby. She rushed up to Miss Martin's desk and helped herself to a big handful of raisins, saying, "Why don't you pass the raisins, Hulda?"

Suddenly a clatter of pounding hoofbeats was heard outdoors. A herd of ten or twelve horses came galloping over the brow of the hill and stopped short. Children and teacher ran out on the porch to see them. The sight was a thrilling one—the horses with arched necks and wild-blown manes silhouetted against the cloudy sky.

"Here, Sugar! Here, Sugar!" called Delores eagerly.

The horses, with one movement, turned their heads and pricked up their ears, looking at the children. But they did not come closer.

"Are they your horses, Delores?" asked Miss Martin.

"Sugar and Nellie are," said the girl. "The others are wild, or else they belong to the neighbors. Sugar and Nellie get wild when they run with them. We had to walk to school this morning—we couldn't catch them."

"They usually come this way ahead of a storm," said Darrell. "We have to chase them home tonight. Looks like they're going over to the Shenkelbergers." The horses were galloping off in the opposite direction.

After a run in the snow, and a first attempt at snowballing, the children came back indoors, their cheeks glowing red from the cold. Delores and Fernetta offered to wash up the lunch dishes. They went out in the kitchen and closed the door. Sixth and seventh grade spelling came first. When Miss Martin asked Emil to spell *sausage,* he spelled *w-u-e-r-s-t* and made the others laugh. All the children knew two languages, but they were ashamed of their German. Suddenly a loud bang was heard in the kitchen and the children laughed louder than ever.

"It's those girls, trying to be fresh," said Jacob Sticklemeyer.

"Go see what's happened, Darrell," said Miss Martin.

Darrell went into the kitchen and looked. "Stovepipe's fell

down," he announced. "Soot all over everything. What we gonna do?"

"Have a minstrel show!" Emil burst out. The boys laughed.

Delores and Fernetta came to the door, their faces and clothes covered with soot. "We weren't doing a thing, Miss Martin," said Delores. "It just came loose of itself."

Everybody ran to the kitchen door to see. The oilcloth-covered table, the floor and the chairs were covered with soot. The rusty stovepipe from the coal-burning Heatola lay in several pieces on the floor.

"We need a new stovepipe," Miss Martin said. "I'm glad I forgot to put more coal on the fire this morning—it's nearly dead. Darrell, take these pieces out, they're rusted clear through."

Darrell took the rusty pipes out to the trash-heap by the barn. Miss Martin stood on the teacherage porch for a moment, and studied the sky. It looked threatening. A great gray blanket of cloud

was pushing forward, and the wind was blowing steadily. It looked as if it might snow heavily.

"The girls will help me clean up the soot," she said, when the boy came back in. "Have you eaten enough lunch, Darrell? Would you take my car and drive to town for me?"

Darrell thought for a minute.

"Heck, Miss Martin, I hate to say no," he replied, "but Delores and I got to get those horses home. Pop will be mad if . . ."

Miss Martin turned to Emil Holzhauer who was gobbling down a final sandwich. Emil was a year older than Darrell, but less responsible.

"Can you go, Emil?" she asked.

"By golly, yes," said Emil, delighted to miss part of a day at school. "In your car? I sure can."

The children went back to their seats, and Miss Martin gave Emil careful instructions.

"Take the car to Schweitzer's garage and tell Ed to winterize it," she said. "Then go to Gustaf Wagner's hardware store and buy new stovepipe for the kitchen. I've written it down, just how much to get. Then go to the Brown Owl and buy these groceries for me." She handed him a written list and a small purse. Then she added in a low voice: "If Holzers have any Christmas trees in yet, buy a nice big one and bring it out."

"A Christmas tree, by golly!" Emil burst out. "Is it time for Christmas?"

The children laughed. They looked at the calendar on the wall. It advertised Wagner's Hardware Store and had a brightly colored picture of a combine on it.

"Why, it's only the fifteenth of November!" cried Delores.

Miss Martin smiled. "I just want to be on the safe side," she said. "The last two years trees have been brought down from Canada in trucks early in the season. They're gone before you know it. It wouldn't be Christmas . . . without a tree." She paused, and Delores thought her eyes looked sad. She turned to Emil again. "If you should see Johannes Wagner, Darrell's father, in town, tell him we're about out of coal."

"I'll tell him at home tonight, Miss Martin," said Delores.

"Jeepers!" exclaimed Emil, as he went out the door. "Hope I can remember everything."

The children watched the car make its way over the hill and disappear, then they went back to their lessons. About half an hour after Emil left, Miss Martin lighted her kerosene lamp and set it on her desk. The room grew gradually darker. Then Darrell asked to go out and look at the weather. When he came in, he said to Delores, "We better get the horses and go home."

"I want to finish my Arithmetic," said Delores. "You fuss like an old mother hen."

"O. K., stay if you want to." Darrell turned to Miss Martin. "I think I better go after our horses."

Miss Martin respected Darrell's weather sense and judgment. "Do as you think best," she said.

The next minute Darrell had his cap and jacket on and was gone. Delores knew the horses had gone over by the Shenkelbergers. That wasn't far. He'd walk over there and ride Nellie home. He'd beat her home sure. But after he left, she couldn't keep her mind on her Arithmetic at all. She wished she had gone with him.

At three o'clock, Pete Hummel, Sr. came in his car for Peter and Hulda. He was a gruff, bewhiskered man with a loud voice. He said the wind was blowing the snow a little. He brought a loaf of bread, a bottle of cream and a slab of bacon. "From the wife," he said.

"Expecting me to be snowbound?" laughed Miss Martin.

"Kids got to eat," he said. "I brought water too. Don't want my kids carryin' water in quart jars, walkin' so far." He put a ten gallon can of water into the front hall.

"When are we going to get the school pump fixed?" asked Miss Martin.

"No use fixin' it," said Pete Hummel, driving off. "Water's alkali."

After the Hummels left, Miss Martin told the other children to go home. "Jacob, go hitch up your horse. You'll walk home, Delores, won't you?"

"Sure!" said Delores. "Man! I wish I'd put on my four-buckle overshoes like Mama told me to."

Konrad Snider rode off on his horse and Jacob Sticklemeyer brought Buckskin and the cart to the front door. All six Sticklemeyer children came running and began to climb in. Delores and Fernetta lifted the twins up. It was snowing more now, and the wind was cold.

"Ruby, is your father coming for you?" asked Miss Martin.

Ruby did not answer. She began to cry.

"Jacob," said Miss Martin, "your cart is full already, but could you squeeze in one more? Ruby could ride part-way with you, then take the short-cut across the prairie."

"Sure, Miss Martin," said Jacob. "We got plenty o' room."

Fernetta held Buckskin's bridle. "Pile in, Ruby," she called. "Buckskin won't know the difference."

With Ruby in, the little cart was overflowing with children. Jacob took the reins and called, "Giddap!" but Buckskin did not move.

He planted his feet firmly and refused to take a step.

"It's you, Ruby," said Fernetta. "Buckskin don't like you. You'll have to get out."

"Oh shoot!" glared Ruby. "I don't care if he likes me or not."

"There's too many, Miss Martin," called Jacob.

"I'll ride on Buckskin's back," said Wilmer, "then Ruby can go with us."

Wilmer climbed on and patted and pounded the horse. But no amount of force or coaxing would make him move. Miss Martin brought a handful of sugar out from the teacherage. Buckskin licked it up, but would not move.

"You'd better wait here at the school, Ruby," said Miss Martin. "Maybe someone will come for you."

"Goody, goody!" cried Ruby. "I hate your old horse, Fernetta, and that crazy old cart's half falling to pieces."

Miss Martin turned to Delores. "Getting the children home every day is such a business, and it's worse after winter really gets here." She waited, but still the Sticklemeyer horse did not go.

"Build a fire under Buckskin," shouted Delores, "and he'll go."

Jacob glared at her and made no reply. He and his brothers and sisters were fond of the stubborn old horse.

"Somebody's coming," called Wilmer. Over the brow of the hill came Sam Englehart on his white horse.

"Oh, goody!" said Ruby. She climbed up behind her father and rode off. Buckskin started to go and the Sticklemeyers waved good-by. Delores went running up the slope. "Good-by, Miss Martin," she called back.

"It's going to storm," answered Miss Martin. "Don't you want to stay here all night?"

Delores remembered the prairie fire and the horses on the night before the first day of school. "No, thank you. I have to go home."

Miss Martin looked lonely, standing there on the teacherage porch, with the snow coming down and the wind blowing her skirt about her. Delores felt suddenly ashamed and disloyal. Miss Martin wanted somebody to be with her. She ought to go back. Then she heard Teacher calling Spike and saw the dog rush up on the porch beside her. Spike would take care of Teacher and the schoolhouse. Spike would keep Teacher from being lonely.

"Tell your father we need more coal," called Miss Martin.

"I will!" Delores shouted back.

She would never forget how her father's horses had thumped around the schoolhouse on the night of the prairie fire. Now they were out in the snow and Darrell was driving them home. Maybe Philip had found them before Darrell got there. Why hadn't she

gone with the boys? She would have had a horse to ride, at least. Now she had to walk all the way home.

It wasn't snowing much, but the wind was getting worse. Blue jeans were never warm, and it was too early to start wearing snow-pants in November. Delores began to run. The wind came against her back. It whipped her coat about her. She tied her scarf more tightly under her chin, put her hands in her pockets and let the wind carry her along.

She thought of Emil Holzhauer on his way to town in Teacher's car. He couldn't drive a car half as well as Darrell could. She wondered when he would get back to the schoolhouse with Miss Martin's stovepipe and groceries. Emil liked to spend the night at his grandparents' in town. He didn't care how much school he missed.

Almost everybody's grandparents lived in town. The old folks had come to the prairie country when they were young. They farmed until they grew old. They were always telling how hard they had worked. They grew old too soon—they couldn't stand hardships any longer. So they moved to town and left the farms to their children and grandchildren.

The walk home seemed twice as far as usual to Delores. Walking south along the railroad track, the wind whipped her from one side and chilled her through. Far ahead in the distance, she could see her father's house and the farm buildings, tiny specks across the whitened prairie. She ran and ran, and got home just as the boys rode in the barnyard with the horses.

"What took you so long?" she yelled.

"They'd left the Shenkelbergers," answered Darrell. "Phil found them clear over to the Holzhauers. Good thing you didn't come with us. You'd be frozen stiff."

"I would not!" Delores answered.

The farmhouse, a story and a half high, stood bleak and unadorned at one side of the barnyard, which was full of farm machinery. There were no shrubs or trees for shelter, so the gaunt structure had taken the punishment of summer heat and winter storms. Heavy posts with cross-arms supported clotheslines across the barren yard. A row of men's overalls whipped up and down in the wind, making a stark pattern against the sky.

The only cheerful note was a light shining from the kitchen window. Delores ran up the back steps, opened the door, turned around and called: "Hurry up, you guys. What makes you so slow?"

Three-year-old Christy came running out.

"Shut that door, Delores," called her mother. "Bring Christy back in."

Christy yelled: "I wanna go see the horses." But Delores pulled him back indoors. She closed the door and stood on the rug that lay just inside. She cleaned the snow off her thin-soled shoes. Christy crawled under the table, and Mama took bread out of the oven. The room had the sweet smell of home-baked bread. It was warm and comfortable.

"Save me the first crust, Mama," said Delores. She went over to the coal range and stood there shivering.

"Look at you now!" scolded her mother. "Your shoes are soaking wet. Take them off quick. Why you not wear your snowpants and overshoes to school like I tell you? When it comes winter, you must dress for winter. All this foolishness like those town girls, wearing only thin cotton jeans without any warm underwear, and ankle socks just to be stylish—I won't have it. Go change your shoes now quick."

Delores slipped her shoes off and left them by the stove to dry. She ran upstairs to change. Just before supper, Papa came home in the truck. He had decided to lease land again for the coming year from Charlie Spotted Bear, the Indian on Oak Creek. He had gone to the Indian Agency in Fort Yates to see about it.

"How are the roads, Johannes?" asked Mama.

"Not bad, not bad," he said. "I slid around a little but come out easy."

"Papa, Miss Martin says the coal at school is about gone," said Delores. "There's not enough to last till Christmas. She told me to tell you. Maybe you like to haul a load over before the roads get bad, hey?"

"Yah, yah," said Johannes. "As if I got no other things to do."

"But at the school, Johannes," began Mama, "with all the little children there. It should be plenty warm. And for Teacher, too— she eats and sleeps there."

"Yah, yah," said Johannes. "First I get coal for my own self, then for Teacher."

"Teacher ordered a Christmas tree already," laughed Delores. "She told Emil Holzhauer if he sees one at Holzers' store, to buy one for the school."

"Christmas trees in November!" snorted Johannes. "All foolishness. These wimmens—always they think up foolishness. It's a long time till Christmas."

Mama put the food on the table and sat down. "Pull up your chairs," she said, as the boys came in. Christy jumped on his mother's lap and began to pound the table with a spoon.

"Yes, wimmens is fools," said Mama. "Every year I say it: the first snow is not so bad. But I know in my heart, and Teacher, she knows too, it is the beginning of the long hard winter."

"Maybe it will snow all night," said Darrell excitedly.

"And blow up drifts as high as the house," added Philip.

"If we can't go to school tomorrow," said Delores, "I'll cry my eyes out."

"Ach! This snow, it is nothing, nothing," said Papa Johannes.

He looked at the three children sitting at the supper table, eating big helpings of beef stew, mashed potatoes and gravy. He looked at fat little Christy on his wife's lap. The children were strong and healthy, and their cheeks were red as apples from the cold air and the snow.

"You boys—you are not babies, I hope?" he said scornfully.

"No, Papa," said Darrell.

"No, Papa," said Philip.

"A little cold weather, then you can take it?"

"Yah, Papa."

"Yah, Papa."

Papa leaned over and pulled a lock of Delores' yellow hair.

"How about you, young lady? You take it too?"

Delores grinned. "Yah, Papa. Sure."

CHAPTER IV

The Christmas Program

"Only nine more sleeps till Christmas!" exclaimed Delores. "Oh, I just can't wait to see what I'm gonna get," said Fernetta. The two girls put their heads together, giggling.

"Jacob drew my name," whispered Delores. "Tell me what he's got for me."

"No, sir, it's a secret," said Fernetta. "But it's something nice."

"Please, Fernetta, please." Delores jumped up and down. "Tell me."

But Fernetta wouldn't. "I bet that old Emil Holzhauer will give me a fly-swatter or something crazy. He's loco!"

The girls burst into peals of laughter.

"Boy! Won't he look purty dressed up in whiskers?"

Emil's head came round the curtain. "Boo!" he shouted. "I'm gonna be Santa Claus and scare the little kids." He held his mask up in front of his face, and the girls tried to snatch it off.

The Oak Leaf children were getting ready for their Christmas program, and had already drawn names for the exchange of gifts. The first snow had long been forgotten. Other snows had come in late November and early December. The prairie was white now, surrounded by snow-topped buttes. Snow was an everyday experience, while overshoes and heavy wraps had become daily necessities.

The program was to be held in the evening, to make it easier for the parents to come. The children worked hard to get ready. They made a big fireplace out of cardboard cartons, and pasted red lined crepe paper on to look like bricks. Darrell made a base for the Christmas tree, bought by Emil long ago in November and kept carefully hidden in the barn until now. Chris Bieber and his wife, Vera Mae, who had no children, brought a battery and a string of lights for the tree. The boys helped string the lights on while the girls stood and admired.

The desks were turned around to face the back of the room. Jacob and Wilmer Sticklemeyer stretched the curtain wire across, and hung the stage curtains on it. This made it possible to use the teacherage kitchen for a dressing room. The Biebers and the Hummels brought lanterns, one for kerosene and the other a gas lantern with a mantle, which made a very bright light.

Evening came all too soon. The people arrived early, as soon as evening chores were done. There were the Hummels, Sniders, Engleharts and the Sticklemeyers, who had children in school, and the

Burgards, Hunstads and Becklers, whose children were grown up now. All the families brought their younger children, who were soon running around the schoolroom. The last ones to arrive were Johannes and Minna Wagner.

"So much to do," complained Mrs. Wagner. "My work, it never gets done." The other mothers nodded their heads in agreement.

"Is it going to snow?" asked Mrs. Englehart. "Ain't it about time for a real good storm?"

"Ach no! We want no storms this winter," said Mrs. Pete Hummel. "I remember a storm once . . ." The talk went on and on.

At eight o'clock, Miss Martin herded the children into her bedroom to put on their costumes.

"I brought my records," said Ruby Englehart. "I got two records to play."

"Delores, has the phonograph come?" asked Miss Martin.

"Darrell drove to town to get it," said Delores. "He'll be here any minute. Ruby's got "Jingle Bells" and "Silent Night.""

Delores was to be Mrs. Santa Claus. She put on her mother's old black silk dress and a little lace cap of Grandma Wagner's. She stood in front of Teacher's mirror in the kitchen and rouged her cheeks and painted her lips. Then she peeped through a hole in the stage curtain, but Darrell wasn't there.

"Jeepers!" she cried. "There's Uncle Gustaf."

He hadn't said a word about coming. He had probably brought Christmas presents for everybody. He always gave her something nice. She wondered what it would be this year. Oh, it was exciting not knowing what anybody was going to give you.

Fernetta Sticklemeyer came out of Teacher's bedroom dressed as Mother Goose and Ruby Englehart as a fairy queen.

"My Mama went to Mobridge last week," Delores whispered to Fernetta. "She brought home a lot of packages and she hid them. I know right where they are—on the top shelf of Mama's closet."

"I got two records already," chimed in Ruby. "My uncle gave them to me."

"Go away," said Fernetta. "We're sick of hearing about those old records of yours. Who cares, anyway?" She turned to Delores. "What do you think is in them?"

"I shook one and it gurgled," said Delores. "Something runny."

Fernetta closed her eyes shrewdly. "Shampoo, maybe? Or a perfume set?"

"I hope it's perfume," said Delores. "But maybe it's for Lavina and not for me. Mama says I'm not old enough."

"She want you to stay a baby?" asked Fernetta.

Delores peeped through the hole again. "Why, there's Darrell. Look, Fernetta, he's talking to Katie Speidel and Norine Schmidt. I bet Uncle Gustaf brought them out from town. They're my best friends—in town, I mean."

Miss Martin sent Peter Hummel out to bring Darrell back of the curtain, but he had no phonograph. "The man wouldn't lend it without a down-payment," said Darrell, "and I didn't have any cash."

"Then you'll have to sing, children," said Miss Martin. " 'Jingle Bells' is the first number."

Hans and Fritz Holzhauer, Emil's older brothers, came to manage the stage curtain. They had graduated from the eighth grade several years before and liked coming back to their old school.

When everybody was ready, the program began. The curtains were pulled back on both sides, and the children sang "Jingle Bells."

Several recitations followed and then it was time for the play *Santa Claus at Home*. In the middle of the performance, Hans Holzhauer dashed back to the kitchen and said, "I'm having trouble. Where's a safety pin?"

"Go look on Teacher's pincushion," whispered Delores.

The curtain had come unhooked from the wire and was sagging badly. Hans hooked it up with a safety pin and the play went on. At the end, the curtains went shut without a hitch and everybody clapped.

After the program came the refreshments. The mothers were always willing to bring food to school, and all had contributed. Every one ate candy and nuts, oranges and cookies. *Halvah* was popular. The Sticklemeyer family brought twelve pounds of the sticky, taffylike candy, all in one piece like a large loaf. Mrs. Sticklemeyer sliced off generous chunks and passed them out. Every child old enough to reach out a hand was eager for *halvah*.

"In the old days we made it ourselves," said Ruby Englehart's grandmother. "Now everybody buys *halvah* at the grocery store."

"What's it made out of, anyhow?" asked Uncle Gustaf Wagner. "Sunflower seeds? It tastes like machine oil to me."

The grown-ups laughed.

"Oh, it's got crushed sesame in it—that's a grain from the old country, and corn syrup, sugar, egg whites and vanilla," explained Grandma Englehart.

"Whatever it's got in it, it sure tastes good to me." Pete Hummel thrust a large bite in his mouth.

"Oh, not so fast!" cried Grandma Englehart. "That's not the way to eat *halvah*. My mother she make me eat it so—first a big bite of bread, then a little bite of *halvah,* then bread again. That way it goes not so fast. It's better for the stummick too."

The others laughed. The room was filled with warmth and friendliness, with good talk and laughter. The children were shrieking and romping with the school dog Spike. Grandpa Englehart was telling a story:

"Never vill I forget! When I turned over that first strip of prairie sod, I remembered that no man had ever touched it before, since the day the good Lord had made it. I tell you then I vas a little scared— and that old Indian watching me too. Never vill I forget vat he said —just three words: 'Wrong side up.' Then he turned his back and walked away."

Nobody said anything. Suddenly the light in a lamp on the window sill flickered. A gust of wind blew in through the broken pane. The lamp flared again and went out. Mrs. Sticklemeyer screamed, and her youngest, little Alvin Calvin, ran to her and began to cry.

Pete Hummel quickly moved the lamp to a safer place. Then he went out the front door, and in a minute was back.

"Hey, folks!" he shouted. "We're gonna have a white Christmas all right. It's snowing hard."

"Snowing—no!" answered the women.

"Looks like a storm comin' up," Pete went on. "Guess we better be gettin' on home."

"Don't tell me it's goin' to be a blizzard," cried Mrs. Sticklemeyer. "I ain't got Adolph's red flannel underwear out yet!"

The others laughed nervously, getting up from their chairs.

"You can't go yet," said Miss Martin, trying to shout above the din. "Santa Claus still has a little work to do. The children haven't had their presents. We drew names and . . ."

"Santa Claus! Santa Claus!" cried the children. "We want our presents." "What you got for us, Santa Claus?"

Emil Holzhauer, wearing his red suit and bearded mask, put his head out from behind the stage curtain and cried: "Hey, wait! Don't go yet. I ain't had my show. What you think we made this crepe-paper fireplace for? Don't you know I got to climb down the chimney and scare the little kids?"

Just then the curtain wire broke and came down. The dog, Spike, barked and pulled at it, and this time a safety-pin was no help at all.

"Come on, we gotta go home," called Pete Hummel again.

"Go home?" cried the women, startled.

Mrs. Englehart had a plate of cookies in one hand and a dish of nuts in the other. Mrs. Hummel was passing out fruit, and Mrs. Wagner was cutting another large three-layer chocolate cake. The refreshments were not half over.

Darrell jumped on a chair in the center of the stage. "Santa Claus hasn't come down the chimney yet," he shouted. "Wait a minute, please . . ."

But no one was listening.

Delores ran to her mother. "Don't let Papa go yet," she said, with her mouth half full of *halvah*. "We've had lots of snowstorms before and we always got home. I want to see what Jacob Sticklemeyer's got for me..."

But Delores could not stop her father. Johannes Wagner said in a loud voice: "There's a storm coming up. Better get home quick, folks."

"Can't we eat first?" cried the boys.

"Don't wait to eat," said Sam Englehart. "Take your food and go home."

"Leave the refreshments for Teacher!" laughed Uncle Gustaf.

"Oh no!" cried Miss Martin. "I'm going to Aberdeen for the holidays. Everything here will get frozen. Take the food with you. Take everything with you. Maybe some of you will take my canned goods, so it won't get frozen while I'm gone."

Like leaves scattering before a wind, the pleasant gathering broke up. Quickly the children thrust presents into each other's hands and in Teacher's. Dishes and food, wraps and small children were collected by the women. Caps, coats, scarves and four-buckle overshoes were hastily put on. Each family took a carton of Miss Martin's canned goods and everybody started to go, calling: "Merry Christmas! Merry Christmas!"

"I want a present from Santa Claus!" wailed little Christy Wagner. Minna wrapped him, screaming, in a blanket and Johannes threw him up over his shoulder.

"Delores, hurry now, get on your wraps. We're going," called Mama Wagner. "Ach, now, what is the matter? What are you crying for?"

"That crazy old Jacob, he didn't give me much—just a stationery, without even pictures on it," sniffed Delores. She opened the small box and showed the note paper to her two girl-friends from town, Kati Speidel and Norine Schmidt, who were waiting for Uncle Gustaf to come.

Miss Martin came running out into the hall and touched Johannes Wagner lightly on the arm. "Mr. Wagner," she said. "We're about out of coal . . . Do you think you could bring some? Before I get back?"

"Yah, yah, sure!" replied Johannes. "I see about it right away, quick, tomorrow. I been too busy to take care of it before."

"You going to town tonight, Miss Martin?" asked Mrs. Wagner.

"Yes," said Miss Martin. "Gustaf said he would take me. I'll leave everything as it is and throw a few things in a suitcase. I'll get the fast train to Aberdeen tomorrow."

Delores saw the worried look in Miss Martin's eyes fade away, as Papa promised to bring the coal. The girl tied her scarf tightly under her chin and buttoned her coat. Miss Martin was still standing there. She had her pretty blue silk dress on, the one she wore to church on Sundays, but no sweater, no wrap, and the front hall was cold with the door standing open. Impulsively, Delores ran to her and threw her arms about her.

"Good night, Miss Martin," she whispered. "Merry Christmas. I hope you have a nice vacation." She followed her parents out into the stormy night.

After the truck engine started, the cab was warm and shielded them from the wind. Only a little snow was falling, but it might get worse in an hour's time. As they rumbled away, Delores looked back and saw the lights in the schoolhouse. She was glad that Uncle Gustaf would drive Miss Martin safely to town.

"Will it be a blizzard, Papa?" asked Delores.

"What? This?" Papa Johannes laughed. "This is nothing."

CHAPTER V

Christmas Vacation

"Papa, you call this nothing?"

It was morning two days later. Delores ran down the steep stairs, through the cold front room and out into the kitchen. She was still in her bathrobe and carried her clothes over her arm. The furnace pipes did not reach to the upstairs bedrooms, and there was no stove, so she was cold. She pointed out the window, where the snow was beating against the house and a high wind was blowing.

"Jeepers! You call this nothing! *I* call it a blizzard."

"This is what Grandpa all the time talks about," said Papa, "the kind they had in the old days, back in 1910."

Darrell came in from the barn, snow-covered. "Here's a snow-storm for you, Delores," he said.

"I don't want it," said the girl. "Keep it for yourself."

Mama had a large frying pan full of sausage on the stove. It was sizzling and sputtering, filling the room with an inviting smell. Delores washed and dressed as quickly as she could. "Where's Christy?" she asked.

"I put him in the boys' bed downstairs," said Mama. "He don't feel so good. He cried all night, and wouldn't let me sleep."

Hearing his name, Christy came out of the bedroom and ran to his mother, crying. She took him up in her arms. Oscar Meyers, the hired man, came in from milking and sat down to eat. Then Darrell came up from the cellar with a coal bucket half full of coal dust.

"How can I shovel coal when there's no coal to shovel?" he demanded.

"I want coal, not that stuff," said Mama. "That's only dust. I got to have *coal* to burn in the kitchen stove."

"There's no coal left," said Darrell.

"No coal?" Papa looked dumbfounded. "Why, I trucked a big load all the way home from Firesteel just last month."

"In October that was," said Oscar.

"We been burning it for three months already," said Mama. "It can't last forever. That furnace is a big hog, the way it eats it up."

Delores said, "There's no coal at school either," but her father did not seem to hear her.

"Fine time to tell me we're out of coal," he shouted, "right in the middle of a big snowstorm. A fine time, I say."

"I've told you a dozen times, Johannes," said Mama, "but always you are too busy. What we going to burn now? The sideboard? Our dresser set we got for our bedroom when we was ten years married?" Mama Wagner was a good-natured woman, but her dark eyes flashed when she was angry. "Get me some wood. No wood—no dinner today."

Johannes ate his breakfast quickly and started toward the back door.

"Wake that lazy Phil up, Darrell," he said, "and you boys come on out. We'll get fuel all right, even in a snowstorm. You come too, Ozzie."

"You tear down the barn for fuel?" Mama called after them. As soon as the door closed, she looked at Delores and laughed. "Your Papa he know he should have got the coal long time ago. He is ashamed, but he won't admit it. It is fun to rub it in a little."

"What'll we burn?" asked Delores, lifting the stove lid. "This fire's going *out*."

"Your Papa, he find fuel all right," chuckled Mama, "and he find it quick, Ozzie will see to that. Get your coat and Christy's and put them on. Bring me my old red sweater."

Delores took Christy on her lap and put his coat on him. She looked out the window and showed him the snow coming down. She was glad it was vacation and she did not have to make the effort to get to school. After Christy jumped down from her lap, she slumped lazily in her chair.

What would she get for Mama for Christmas? She wanted something nice this year. But with all this snow, when would she be able to go to town? The snow wasn't coming *down* at all. It was coming sideways, straight from the north, pushed along by the wind. In some places the ground was swept clean. In other places, drifts were piling up against the farm machinery which stood in the barnyard. The wheels of the tractor were half-covered already.

"If the tractor costs so much money," asked Delores, "why don't Papa take care of it and put it in the barn? It's getting snowed under, and so are the plows and the drill and the disc and the drag and both the combines."

"How big a barn you think we got?" asked Mama. After washing up the dishes, she started preparations for dinner. "I was going to bake bread today, but how can I with no fuel?"

Christy ran to his mother and hung on her apron. He coughed and his nose was running.

"Hold him, Delores," said Mama. "Keep him out from under my feet."

Delores held Christy again. "Listen!" she said. The sound of sawing and chopping could be heard. "They're chopping, Mama."

"Ach!" laughed Mama. "The railroad ties—I thought so. We are lucky we have land on both sides of the railroad track, so we have plenty of ties. Sawing ties—that will be good exercise for a cold day."

Discarded railroad ties had been left along the tracks by the section men who kept the road in repair. In return for plowing a fire-guard two furrows wide along the track, the farmers were allowed to take the ties. Johannes Wagner had hauled a large pile into the barnyard and unloaded them by the chicken coop. He intended to build a "tie shed" out of them, posts and supports covered with straw, for shade for the cattle in summer and protection from snow in winter. But now he had to use them for fuel.

The door soon opened and Darrell and Philip brought in big armfuls of chopped wood, sawed chunks of ties split for the stove.

"Make us a good hot dinner, Mom," begged Darrell.

"I'll think about it," said Mama.

"We had to shovel all the way to the chicken coop," said Darrell.

"Jeepers!" complained Philip. "No fun sawin' wood with snow blowin' up in your face." The boys hurried out again.

"Delores, you scrub the floor," said Mama. "I'll go down cellar and see if I can find something to eat. The cellar's so cold, I'm afraid my canned stuff will freeze."

Delores swished the mop over the linoleum and Christy crawled in the puddles of water she made. Mama came upstairs with a basket full of canned goods. She set the jars on the floor back of the stove.

"Make Christy stay out of the water, Mama," said Delores.

"Mama, take me up," screamed Christy. "Gimme candy. Buy me candy bar."

Mama picked the boy up and held him on her lap. She sat down in the kitchen rocker and rocked until he fell asleep. Then she put him back to bed in the side room again. At noon, she made macaroni salad, boiled potatoes and opened canned chicken. Papa and Oscar and the boys ate quickly and went out again. The house got colder and colder. There seemed to be no let-up in the storm.

In the afternoon, Chris Bieber appeared on his tractor, bringing cousin Reinhold Wagner. Reinhold was a tall, lanky town boy, sixteen years old, Uncle August's son. Uncle August ran a barber shop in town.

"I came to spend Christmas vacation on the farm," laughed Reinhold.

"You brought us a fine storm from town," said Delores.

Chris Bieber was a neighbor who lived two miles from the Wagners. "I was in town buyin' groceries," he said, "and I ran into

Reinhold. He was crazy to get out to the farm, and his Pop wouldn't bring him, so I did." He turned to Mrs. Wagner. "Got any coal?"

"What? You folks out too?" Minna laughed.

"Vera Mae's been givin' me heck," said Chris. "I thought Johannes and I could take his truck to town and get some coal for both of us."

"Fine time you pick for hauling coal," grinned Delores.

"Where's the men-folks?" asked Chris.

"Out sawin' railroad ties," said Minna. "The furnace is out and the house is cold. No coal even for the kitchen range. We're burning tie wood today."

Chris Bieber laughed. "Reiny, guess we better go help."

By nightfall, the cellar had wood in it, and the downstairs was warm from a wood fire in the furnace. Even though he knew his wife, Vera Mae, would worry, Chris Bieber stayed all night, so he could help get the coal in the morning.

When morning came, it was still snowing. After an early breakfast, Johannes said: "Ozzie, you take the tractor and the hayrack and go out to the stacks and get a load of hay. Here's three big boys to help you. Clear the snow off one of the stacks and drive the range cattle down there to eat. Bring a load of hay back to the barn for the saddle-horses and milk-cows. Don't know how long this storm will last. Phil, you can drive the tractor part of the way for Ozzie. Reiny and Darrell, you'll have to shovel some."

"Oh boy! Shovel some? I'll say so," said Darrell.

"Yippee!" exclaimed Reiny. "I been dyin' to buck a few drifts."

"Criminy sakes!" growled Philip. "I'd like to stay in and keep warm. What we got a warm house for?"

"Come on, boys," called Oscar, opening the door.

"Can I go with the boys, Papa?" asked Delores. "I can shovel some."

"Nope, you stay in and help your Mama," said Papa. "You know how she gets in a storm like this. Try and keep her cheered up."

"Oh shoot!" cried Delores. "The boys get to have all the fun."

"Ain't you comin' with us, Pop?" asked Darrell.

"Nope, Chris and I are taking his tractor and my truck and we're goin' after a load of coal," said Papa Wagner. "We got to load the truck with wheat, to hold it down on the road. No tellin' when we'll get back."

After the boys and men left the house, Delores was left alone with her mother and little brother.

"The men'll get in a ditch," sighed Mama, "and the boys'll never make it. The stacks are two miles away across the prairie. They'll have to shovel every inch."

"Don't you worry none," said Delores. "They'll make it all right."

The house was quiet now except for Christy's coughing. Delores went down cellar and filled the furnace with wood, then into the front room to listen to the battery radio. It was still cold there, with the northwest wind blowing around the corner. She had to put both coat and snowpants on to keep from shivering.

"You come out of that cold room," called Mama. "You'll catch cold."

"Just a minute," said Delores. "It's time for the news—maybe I can get the weather report. If it stops snowing, we'll go to town tomorrow and I'll do my Christmas shopping."

The radio sputtered, but the battery was not dead. Delores could hear what the man was saying:

". . . bad storm over the Great Plains . . . from Nebraska to

Montana . . . cattle and sheep drifting before the storm . . . huddled in fence corners beneath the drifts . . . miles from their home ranges . . . wet snow . . . freezing on their eyes, ears and bodies . . . many reported dead . . ." That was all. It faded out again.

Alarmed, the girl ran to the kitchen.

"The cattle are freezing to death," she cried. "The man said the drifts are getting so high they are burying the cattle and they can't get out."

"Ach! So!" cried Mama. "That must be north of here, up in Canada."

"He said in Nebraska," replied Delores. "That's south of here."

"Nebraska!" exclaimed Mama. "They always get bad blizzards in Nebraska. I always read it in the paper."

"We better put our cattle in the barn, Mama," said Delores, "before they freeze to death."

Mama laughed. "How big a barn you think we got, hey? First you put all the farm machinery in, and now seventy head of range cattle. What you think? You talk like a dumb town girl."

"Don't they get cold staying out all winter long, with no food and no shelter?" asked Delores.

"Some of them die," said Mama sadly. "One winter they all died —three thousand dollars we lost. Plenty farmers lose their whole herd. Even if they live through the winter, they're poor skinny creatures by spring." Mama brought out her sewing basket and a pile of clothes to mend.

"If the hay lasts out," she said, "they'll live. That is, if they can get to the stacks. In a storm like this, they start going with the wind at their backs, and they keep going till they get stopped by a fence and get banked up against it, or till they all get drowned in a creek.

The Herefords are the best ones to nose the snow away and try to eat the prairie grass underneath, like the horses do. The others got to get to the stacks." Mama sewed quietly, then she added, "When summer comes, they eat grass again and grow strong."

"I don't see why Pop couldn't let me go out," said Delores. "I'm stronger'n Darrell is. I can throw him wrastling."

"You'd go off and leave me here alone?" said Mama. "Go get your embroidery and do a little work on it."

Delores brought out her dresser scarf, replaced the embroidery hoops, and started to work on the design of wild roses.

"Jeepers!" she cried impatiently. "My thread always gets knots in it."

Mama did not answer. Her face looked sad. The needle and thread in her hand went steadily up and down. The kitchen grew dark as the afternoon wore on. Christy was sleeping on the bed in the next room. He stirred restlessly and began to cough. Mama put down her mending when she could no longer see.

"Light the lamp, Delores," she said. "Did you clean the chimney?"

"Criminy, no," said the girl. "I forgot."

"Go do it quick then."

Delores washed the blackened lamp chimney and polished it with a dry, clean cloth.

"It gets dark early in a storm," said Mama. "Is plenty oil in all the lamps?"

"Yah, I filled them full," said Delores. "Now if we had electricity—"

"If we had electricity," Mama interrupted sternly, "we would have no light at all. The people in town have no lights when the storms come. Lavina tells me so, and Grandma Wagner and Mrs. Thiel and all the ladies. In town they sit in darkness till the storm is over. They eat cold food and sit in a cold kitchen. Electric stoves do not burn wood." Mama got up and put more wood on the fire.

"I wish we had a pretty little house like Grandma's just the same," said Delores. She jerked her embroidery thread impatiently.

Mama sighed. "The house must wait—so your Papa says. The farm machinery must first be paid for. Last year a new tractor and a new truck too. All this machinery, it eats up all the money."

"Why do we buy so much?"

"Oh, the men—the men, they put their heads together, they say they got to have more and more."

Delores looked out the window. "Everything's white," she said. "I can't see a thing but a white blur. Blizzards are so white."

"Except when they are black," said Mama.

"Black!" said Delores. "Whoever heard of a black blizzard?"

"I have *seen* one," said Mama. "I have seen plenty of them and tasted them too."

She went into the bedroom to look at Christy. She put her hand on his head, and came back, shaking her own.

"The baby is sick," she said, "and at a time like this."

"What's a black blizzard?" asked Delores.

"Sand, dirt, gravel blowing up and hitting you in the face instead of clean snow," said Mama, sitting down in the rocker. "You are too young. It was before you were born, in the thirties—1935, 1936 and 1937."

"Oh, the dust storms," said Delores. "We studied about them in school. But I didn't know they happened here. I thought they were in Kansas and Nebraska."

"Yes, and here too, in the Dakotas," said Mama. "The wind don't stop at the state line. They were all over the Great Plains from Texas to Montana. The Sioux Indians say the prairie grass should never have been broken up. Maybe they are right. Maybe the first settlers shouldn't have broken the sod and planted big fields of wheat. When so many dry summers came in a row, the wind blew day and night and whoof—the air was full of dirt. It blew in our eyes, our noses, our throats, our lungs. Many died of tuberculosis, children too. Ach! The hard time, the trouble, the sickness . . . five years in a row we made no crop . . . not a blade of wheat came up. Ach! it was terrible . . ." Tears came in Minna Wagner's eyes, as she looked out the window.

"I don't like the snow," she said. "I don't like the wind. But whenever I see a white blizzard blowing, I thank God it is not a black one." Christy began to cough in the bedroom. "Bring him to me," said Mama.

Delores carried the boy out and put him in his mother's lap. Christy, usually so full of life and spirit, was limp and sickly now.

"He's had fever all day," said Mama. "And on such a day we run out of coal and have a cold house."

"The boys—why do they stay so long?" said Delores. "Soon it will be dark."

"In warm weather, they can chase the cattle down to the stacks," said Mama. "But now the stacks are covered with snow. They must shovel all that long way."

"Does Christy need a doctor?" asked Delores.

"All summer, all fall, we run to town two-three times a week for nothing at all," Mama said. "All summer, we go twice a week to take you kids to the show. What is a show when a baby lies sick of the fever?"

Delores stood beside her mother, looking down at her little brother.

"So many times we run," Mama went on, "we use gas, we have the old car, the truck, the tractor. We can take one or the other and run off to town. We can run in after supper and get home before bedtime. Nine miles—it is nothing. But in the winter time, when the big blizzard comes, and the baby lies sick, there is no car to take him to the doctor."

"The old car—it's broke down," said Delores.

"Oh yes, the old car, it's broke down, it's got a flat tire, it's got this and that wrong with it," said Mama, "and the truck and the tractor, they are gone."

The tears ran down Mama's cheeks, and Delores could not bear to see it. She wanted to cheer her up but she did not know how.

"What for? What is all this machinery for?" There was despair in Mama's voice. "Always more and more machinery to get out of

order, to break down when we need it most. The men are not farmers any more. They are mechanics, and poor ones at that."

Delores got up and put more wood on the stove.

"Maybe Christy will be better tomorrow," she said. "What'll we fix for supper?"

"I'm making sour *knipfla*," said Mama. "Are the potatoes done?"

"Yah," said Delores, trying them with a fork.

"The roll of dough is ready," said Mama. "Take the scissors and cut little pieces off and put them into the potato-and-water mixture. Let it cook till the *knipfla* get done. Then I'll put the sour cream and vinegar in."

Suddenly a rush came against the outside door. The dog, Rover, barked and a scuffle was heard. The door burst open, and in rushed the three boys, followed by the hired man.

"Shut the door! Shut the door quick!" called Delores. "Brush that snow off outside."

"Jeepers!" cried Darrell. "It's nice and warm in here. My cheek's frozen. Let me get it thawed out." He brought in a panful of snow and held handfuls up to his cheek.

"Did you get some hay?" asked Mama, as she put Christy back to bed.

"No," said Oscar. "Pretty big job gettin' hay in weather like this."

"Got stuck a dozen times," said Phil. "Had to unhitch the hay-rack and leave it out there. Maybe we can drive the cattle up to it tomorrow and let them eat."

"Tractor was always gettin' stuck and we had to dig it out," said Reiny.

"The snow blew up in our faces and then froze," said Darrell. "We had to stop and pull the ice from our eyes and warm our hands

on the exhaust from the tractor. We couldn't see the road ahead
of us."

"Jeepers!" exclaimed Delores. "Wish I could have been out. You
guys have all the fun."

"Fun?" cried Reiny and Philip. "It was work and we're hungry."

"Go take off those wet clothes," said Mama, "then we'll eat. We
won't wait for Papa. No tellin' when he'll get here."

"Why is it so quiet?" asked Darrell. "Where's Christy? Where's
my little pal? I want to have a boxing match with him."

"He's a pretty sick boy," said Mama, pointing to the bedroom.

"Jeepers!" Darrell shook his head. "What a Christmas vacation!"

CHAPTER VI

Coal for Christmas

When morning came, Delores ran to the window the first thing. "Well, I'll be jiggered," she said, "If it ain't still blizzarding."

"A peach of a snowstorm for you, Delores!" cried Darrell at breakfast.

"This one's yours, not mine," retorted Delores.

"If only the wind would die down," said Cousin Reinhold, "we could go out and play Fox-and-Geese."

"Go find an Eskimo to play with," said Delores. "Criminy sakes, but the house is cold."

"Where's Pop and Chris Bieber?" asked Darrell.

"Ach! They never got back at all," said Mama. "All night I could not sleep one wink. What if they ran in a ditch and got buried deep in the snow?"

"Big strong men can dig themselves out," said Oscar Meyers.

"Darrell, go build up the furnace fire," said Mama. "That tie wood burns out overnight. That's why it's so cold."

Reinhold stepped out on the back porch and came quickly in again. "Golly! It's twenty-seven below," he said.

"Jeepers!" exclaimed Phil, shivering beside the stove. "Twenty-seven degrees too cold for me. Zero's bad enough."

"And tomorrow's Christmas," sighed Delores. "A fine Christmas it will be. No presents, and Mom without sugar and cake flour to make a cake."

"I wasn't gonna fix much," said Mama. "I thought we was goin' in to Grandma Wagner's. But even if Christy was well, we could never get there now."

Delores stood by the window. "If it would just stop snowing . . . we could go after all. Then if the stores were still open . . ." She remembered she hadn't bought a thing for Mama for Christmas.

"We'd better forget about it," said Mama. "If we get coal for Christmas, we'll be lucky. And Pop back safe. That'll be Christmas for me."

After breakfast, Oscar and the boys went out to tackle the hay-stacks again. Delores went into the front room and turned on the battery radio. She listened a while, then came back to the kitchen. She sat down and began to work on her embroidery.

"Mama, the man on the radio told how to signal for an airplane."

"Airplane!" said Mama with scorn. "With such contraptions I

will have nothing to do. The tractors—they give us enough trouble. All they do is break down."

"Teacher is not afraid of airplanes," said Delores. "She took a ride with Paul Kruger in his plane once. He flew her all the way from town out to Oak Leaf School after the Fair. She said she felt like she had wings on, herself!"

Mama shook her head. "Such foolishness!"

"The man said a big circle or a plus-sign tramped in the snow would signal a plane to land here," Delores went on. "He said to make an F for food, and a double XX for doctor or medicine."

"All foolishness," said Mama. "What good to make a sign when the wind blows like sixty and covers it right up?"

"He said to spread ashes," replied Delores. "I can go in the cellar and shovel some . . ."

"Delores Wagner!" exclaimed Mama. "Are you then so dumb? Who of us is starving? Are we then out of food? Look at all the eggs. Look there back of the stove at all my jars of canned stuff. Are we then starving?"

"No, not yet," said Delores hastily. "But we're out of sugar, and you said you used the last of the coffee this morning. Other people are out of food. One family had only macaroni to eat for three days, because they couldn't get to the store. They got sick and tired of it."

"Poor sort of people," sniffed Mama, "if they had no home-canned stuff and no root vegetables in their cellar."

"He said all their meats and vegetables were in frozen food lockers in town," said Delores. "And they couldn't get to town."

"Frozen food lockers," sniffed Mama. "Such new-fangled notions. What's the matter with their own cellar?"

"But you had to bring all our stuff up from the cellar, to keep it from freezing," said Delores. "Over the radio, they told about a man who froze to death and the snow covered his body. Just his feet were sticking out. They had to bring a bulldozer to dig him out of the snow."

"Ach! Tell me not such awful things, when Johannes has been gone so long," wailed Mama.

"The airplanes are dropping bales of hay to the cattle, and they are taking sick people to the hospital," Delores went on. "I bet if Paul Kruger knew . . ."

"Who of us is freezing or dying?" asked Mama. "Only Christy has a sore throat. You think I don't know how to take care of him? Let the airplane go to those who are in need."

But by noon, Mama herself was worried. Christy was not getting better and she had used up all the medicine. She brought the little boy out and held him in her arms in the rocking chair. "If only I could get that prescription filled, and some more cough medicine . . ."

"I wish we had a telephone," said Delores. "We could call Paul Kruger up and ask him to bring it out."

"The farmhouses are too far apart for stretching telephone wires," said Mama. "If Darrell was here, he could go on Nellie. All the coffee is gone and there are only a few matches left . . ."

"The cattle wouldn't get their hay, if the boys went," said Delores. "Why can't I go to town? I can ride better than Darrell."

"You? A little girl like you?" cried Mama, horrified. "Every year we read in the paper about little girls getting lost in the deep snow. You think I'm crazy enough to let you go?"

"Now Mama, don't be silly," said Delores. "The radio says

the worst of the storm is over. You know the first three days of a storm are always the worst, and this is the third day. Uncle Rudolph would be out to his farm today, Mama, doing his chores. He comes out every other day about one o'clock to feed his cattle. It was storming so bad yesterday, I don't suppose he ever came. He'd be sure to come today."

Mama nodded, but did not say anything.

"If I could get over to Uncle Rudolph's barn," said Delores, "I could go to town with him in his jeep."

"Are you crazy, girl?" cried Mama. "How you gonna get there, anyhow?"

"Ride a horse," said Delores. "Old Nellie's got plenty sense. She won't go where it's not safe. Its no worse than riding to school. If it was school you'd *make* me go."

It took a lot of coaxing. Only because Christy was getting worse did Mama finally consent. "I'll let you go as far as Uncle Rudolph's," she said.

"O. K., Mama," said Delores. She ran to get ready.

"You put on two pairs of jeans under your snowpants," said Mama, "and a sweater under your coat. Get a wool scarf for your head."

"Oh, Mama, you'd like to dress me up like an Eskimo," laughed Delores. "You'd think I was making an expedition to the North Pole. I'm not Admiral Byrd. It's only four miles to Uncle Rudolph's."

"Four miles in a storm is twice as far as in fair weather," said Mama. "If you see smoke at the Hunstad's place, stop there and rest."

"Yah, Mama. Sure." Delores started out the door, with the doctor's prescription and grocery list in an inside pocket.

"You'll be lucky to find Uncle Rudolph there," said Mama. "If he's not, you turn right around and come home. I'll send Papa to town after he comes with the coal."

"I hate to leave you alone, Mama," said Delores.

"Pooh! You go along, you!" Mama tried to laugh, but her eyes were wet.

Delores was glad to get out, even if the snow was still blowing and the wind icy cold. It was better than being cooped up inside. She shoveled a drift away to get into the barn. Sugar nickered and wanted to go, but Delores knew the larger horse, Nellie, would be better. When she came out of the dark barn on Nellie's back, she had to squint because the snow was so bright. Over in the east the sky looked lighter.

It took a long time to get to Uncle Rudolph's. After crossing the railroad track, Nellie chose her own path, walking where there was least snow, often up to her belly. When the drifts became deeper, Delores got off and led the horse, kicking a path with her feet. The wind swept across the prairie with terrific force, and she was glad she had worn so many clothes. But walking was not easy for her or for the horse.

"Jeepers!" She said to herself. "At this rate, it will take me all day."

At last she came within sight of the Hunstad place, a small farmhouse with a windbreak of trees, on the banks of Oak Creek. Smoke was pouring from the chimney, which meant that the hired man must be staying there to look after the cattle. She knew that the Hunstads lived in town in the winter. It was too hard to lead Nellie all the way to Uncle Rudolph's. Delores wondered if she could leave her in the Hunstad's barn. She went to the back door and knocked.

The hired man, nicknamed Whiskers, opened the door a crack, and peeped out, unshaven, with a pipe in his mouth.

"Yah, yah!" he nodded in answer to her question. "Sure mike! That's O. K. Put your horse in the barn. It makes me no difference out."

He did not notice that the girl was cold. He did not ask her to come in, or offer to help. The kitchen door was quickly closed to keep the heat in and the cold out. Delores had no chance to say that she would like to come in and rest awhile.

She managed to get the barn door open, and found an empty stall and some oats for Nellie. It was only a mile now to Uncle Rudolph's. She could make better time without the horse. If she could only catch Uncle Rudolph there, doing his chores . . . She hated to think what she would do if he was not there. There was

no house at his place, only a barn and straw shed.

The mile was long and the snow in Oak Creek valley was deep. The girl trudged wearily on. Uncle Rudolph's barn was a long way from the road which circled a hill. It stood in a low flat place near a bend in Oak Creek. She walked faster. After the sun came out, the snow blinded her, and she could not see which way she was going.

Ach! There he was! She could see Uncle Rudolph's jeep by the barn and his cattle under the straw shed. How happy she felt. A jeep could go anywhere, even on drifted roads. How lucky! Had he just come, or was he ready to leave? If he was leaving, could she ever catch him? Would he see her waving or hear her call? If she missed him, she would have to walk to town, five more miles. She tried to run and stumbling, fell headlong. She lay there for a minute, resting, then pulled herself to her feet.

She saw a man come out of the barn and she knew it was Uncle Rudolph. He was just going away in his jeep. She called and waved frantically. The jeep started, then it stopped. It started up again, and this time, turned and came toward her. Just as she had hoped, Uncle Rudolph had seen her. He came as close as he could, then stopped and waited till she came up.

"What's the matter?" he asked. "Where you goin'? Anything wrong?"

"Christy's bad sick," said Delores. "I got to get medicine at the drugstore in town. Pop's haulin' coal and the boys are gettin' hay, so there's no one to go but me. Will you take me in the jeep?"

"Sure as shootin'," said Uncle Rudolph. "Pile in."

It was better luck than Delores had hoped for. She gave a sigh of relief. The jeep rocked her from side to side, but being shaken up was better than walking. The jeep had side-curtains too, which kept off the wind. It had chains on all four wheels, so it crawled over snowbanks four and five feet high. It moved slowly but surely and at last reached Yellowstone Trail, where other cars had left tracks. From there on, the going was easy. But because of the late start, it was nearly dark when they reached town.

"You stay at Lavina's tonight," said Uncle Rudolph. "I'll pick you up at the trailer-house first thing in the morning and take you home."

Delores hurried to the grocery. The streets were emptier than she had ever seen them. The snowplow had pushed high banks of snow into the gutters. The sidewalks had not been shoveled, but were tramped down in a narrow path. Delores bought coffee, matches and five pounds of sugar at the grocery first, then just got into the drugstore before it closed. She had Christy's prescription filled and bought a bottle of cough syrup. By the time she came out, the other stores were closed. In Holzers' window she saw a beautiful nut-cracker set, a wooden bowl with nut-picks and a cracker. She looked at it longingly, but could not get in to ask the price.

"Oh, dear," she thought. "Now I haven't got a thing for Mama for Christmas."

The lights shone brightly from the little blue trailer-house, and were a sign of welcome as the girl came stumbling up the street through the snow. She pounded on the door and Lavina opened it.

"Criminy sakes!" cried Lavina. "First Pop, then you—on a day like this. Where did you drop from—out of an airplane?"

"Uncle Rudolph brought me in his jeep." Delores dropped her packages and sank on the couch, exhausted. For a while she could not talk. "I got a pain in my side," she whispered.

"Here, drink this cup of coffee," said Lavina. "You look white as a sheet. This will warm you up inside and rest you."

Lavina had a good supper ready and after Delores had eaten, she felt better. Melvin came in and Delores told them her whole story. "Now tell me about Pop," she said.

"Pop stopped in after he got his coal loaded up," said Lavina. "He and Chris Bieber had dinner at Grandma's. I knew you folks would never be able to get into Grandma's for Christmas tomorrow, so I bought some groceries for Mama and a little Christmas. Grandma sent over her Christmas treats for all you kids."

"You started out to our place?" asked Delores.

"Yah, twice, but had to turn back," said Lavina. "Mel was afraid of the roads. I tried to find Paul Kruger with his airplane, to take the stuff out, but they said he was bringin' a sick woman in to the hospital."

"Mama won't have anything to do with airplanes," said Delores. "She says they break down as easy as tractors."

"Oh, Mama!" laughed Lavina. "She's always the last one to catch onto a new style. Remember her bobbed hair? We'll get her in an airplane yet. Boy! Was I ever glad to see Pop. What do you think? *He* bought a box of groceries for Mom too—the very same stuff I bought. I made him take everything out on his coal truck, but he went off without the Christmas tree."

"I'll take it," said Delores, "and then we'll have a tree—at least."

Delores slept soundly with Lavina's twins. On Christmas morning, she was stiff all over and felt very tired, but Uncle Rudolph came to the door early. She drank a cup of coffee and ate a piece of summer sausage for her breakfast. She put her bundles and the little evergreen tree in the back of the jeep, then climbed in.

It was a beautiful Christmas day. The blizzard was over and the sun came out in all its brilliance, to make the snow shine and sparkle. Uncle Rudolph took Delores as far as the Hunstads, then hurried back to town to have Christmas with his family. At the Hunstads, the girl put her groceries in a feed sack and tied the Christmas tree to her saddle. She did not go into the house and Whiskers, the hired man, did not come out. She rode across the prairie, following her path of the previous day, where it was still visible.

"Here comes our Christmas tree girl!" Mama met her at the door and gave her a tight hug.

"Lavina sent the tree, Mama," said Delores. "Ain't it pretty?"

"Ach! You are home safe again," said Mama. "I was sick with worry when you did not come home last night. Poor Christy, he could hardly breathe. I ran the steam kettle all night for his cough.

I never once took my clothes off even."

"I got the prescription filled just before the drugstore closed."

"Good," said Mama. "Soon he will be better."

"Jeepers! Is the house ever hot!" exclaimed Delores. "Must be, Papa brought the coal."

"Yah, at last," said Mama. "They got stuck three times and had to walk back to town to get Schweitzer's wrecker to come pull them out. They took half the load over to Biebers, so Vera Mae could have a warm house for Christmas too."

"And the boys?"

"They finally got a load of hay to the barn, and the cattle came in," said Mama. "Poor kids—that is work for men, not for boys. That Ozzie, he's only nineteen—just a kid too."

"Mama!" exclaimed Delores, remembering. "Papa's got to get coal for school too."

"Yah, I told him," said Mama, "and he said there is plenty time for that."

"He better not wait too long," said Delores.

Soon Papa and the boys came tramping in.

"Merry Christmas!" shouted Papa. "They tell me it's Christmas!"

While Mama was preparing and roasting the duck for Christmas dinner, Delores set the little evergreen tree on the sideboard in the front room. Darrell hung shiny balls and tinsel on it. Mama brought her packages out from their hiding place and laid them under it. After dinner, Mama got Christy out of bed and held him on her lap to see the tree. Delores heated the iron and pressed her wild rose dresser scarf. It was all she had to give to Mama.

"Jeepers! Is the house ever hot!" cried the boys.

Once the lignite coal in the furnace was well started, it made the house too warm. The family threw off sweaters and coats.

"It's like summer, hey?" Papa chucked Mama under her double chin.

"Come on, let's open the presents," begged the boys.

"What Santy Claus bring me?" asked Christy. "Candy bar?"

The gurgling package was perfume, just as Delores expected. She got a new blue sweater and a pocketbook too. Mama gave her a kiss for the dresser scarf, and said wild roses were her favorite flower. Ozzie and the boys got plaid wool shirts and Christy a toy dump-truck. After admiring all the presents, they all ate *Kaffeekuga* and drank hot coffee.

Then came Grandma Wagner's treats—a paper sack for each grandchild which contained one orange, one apple, nuts, cookies, Russian peanuts, a candy bar and a popcorn ball. Grandma sent a new tie for Papa Johannes and for Mama a pretty pincushion crocheted on the wishbone of a chicken.

At the last minute, Papa tossed a small box into Mama's lap. When Mama opened it, they all gathered round and gasped in astonishment. It was a pretty gold wristwatch on a gold-chain bracelet.

"Well, I never!" exclaimed Mama. The kiss she gave Papa was a resounding smack. "Look at me here now, with this! A wristwatch! Don't that beat the Dutch! And I thought I was lucky to get *coal for Christmas!*"

CHAPTER VII

The Lasso Rope

"Hey, Darrell! Konrad! Bet you can't catch us!" cried Peter Hummel. "All three of us."

Peter, Hulda and Ruby ran in three different directions across the prairie, which was the play-yard of the school. Darrell chased after them, lasso rope in hand.

"I'll catch Peter," he called. "You get the two girls, Konrad."

A minute later, the two big boys had captured the three younger children and had tied the long rope in loops and knots around them in a squirming mass.

"Now, you're hog-tied!" said Darrell.

"We're hog-tied! We're hog-tied!" they repeated. They tumbled on the ground in a helpless heap, roped together, laughing as hard as they could.

Ding dong! Ding dong! Delores stood at the schoolhouse door and rang the bell.

"It's time for school to take up," said Ruby. "How we gonna get loose?"

"Konrad, come and untie us," called Peter.

But Konrad ran in, and it was Delores who came and untied all the knots. "Bring Teacher's lasso rope inside," she said to Peter.

"That's not Teacher's lasso rope," said Ruby. "It's my jump rope. I brought it from home."

"You never!" said Delores sharply. "This is Teacher's rope. Your old jump rope's a short one. It caused so much trouble, Teacher told you to take it home. You took it home your own self."

"I brought it back again," said Ruby sullenly.

"Well, this is not it," said Delores. "Teacher bought this one at my Uncle Gustaf's hardware store in town. See how long it is— thirty feet. Reason why I know is, my Uncle Gustaf told my Pop that Teacher asked for twelve feet, and thought that was long enough for a lasso rope."

"Huh! Shows how little she knows!" sniffed Ruby.

"She comes from the East River country," said Delores. "That's why she don't know any better. She never rode horses or lassoed cattle in her life. She can't help it. You don't need to blame her. My uncle sold her thirty feet instead of twelve. Was your rope thirty feet long, Ruby Englehart?"

Ruby hesitated. "I guess not . . ."

"Hurry, children," called Miss Martin. They came running in.

"Hang the lasso rope here in the hall and take off your wraps."

Christmas vacation, with the first bad blizzard of the winter, was over. Delores was glad to be back in school again. There had been no snow since New Year's, but the weather still stayed cold. She and Darrell had come together on Sugar.

"Our horse didn't want to come to school today," said Delores. "She kept trying to turn around and go back. Don't know what got into her."

"It's a good thing our blizzard didn't come at New Year's, Miss Martin," said Darrell. "You'd a been stalled in Aberdeen."

"In the real bad blizzards, all the trains stop running on the main line," said Emil Holzhauer, "even the flyer, that Olympian Hiawatha too, headed for Seattle, Washington. Diesel engines are no good in blizzards."

"I was lucky to get back to Oak Leaf safely," said Miss Martin. "My train was on time, and the road out here was frozen hard, so I had no trouble with my car. I wonder how long it will be before I get to town again . . . Our big snows always come in January and February."

"Maybe we'll have a warm winter this year," said Peter Hummel.

"A warm winter!" All the children laughed.

Although none of them realized that the worst winter in the history of the Great Plains was ahead of them, every West River child knew that winter could never be warm. Winter was a rugged battle to be fought and endured. Seven-year-old Peter knew it as well as the others.

"Don't you fool yourself!" laughed Darrell. "I can feel it in my bones, this winter's gonna be a humdinger. It hasn't got a good start yet."

"I'm prepared for the worst," said Miss Martin solemnly. "Hans Holzhauer rode up to my back door yesterday and brought me a big loaf of homemade bread..."

"Hans Holzhauer?" asked Delores.

"Hans is one of my old boys," said Miss Martin. "He never forgets his old school or his old teacher. He likes to come and sit down and visit ever so often. And Sam Englehart brought back one of my boxes of canned goods—the box he kept over Christmas for me."

"Then we won't starve," said Konrad Snider.

"*Our* daddy brought you a can of water this morning," said Peter Hummel, smiling proudly.

"So we won't get thirsty," added Hulda.

"And a box of spuds," added Peter.

"So we won't get hungry," said Hulda.

All the children were glad to be back in school again. It was a change from the isolation at home during the stormy holidays. They showed a lively interest in their lessons and Miss Martin was pleased. Since there were no story or reference books in their homes, they enjoyed looking things up in the school dictionary or encyclopedia. And they liked reading the story books borrowed by mail from the county and state libraries.

The day passed happily and busily. It began to snow in the afternoon, but no one thought anything of it. Snow came every day. It was as inevitable as morning and night. Just before the afternoon recess, the wind began to blow hard from the east. The large east windows of the schoolroom, never too tight, began to rattle.

"The wind sounds like someone screaming!" giggled Fernetta

Sticklemeyer. "Screaming at the top of their voice!"

"No," said Konrad Snider. "It's more like a siren. I heard a fire engine when I was in Aberdeen once." He began to imitate the sound.

"Oh, stop it!" cried Darrell Wagner. "It's bad enough to have the wind whistling outside. We don't need it inside too."

For the afternoon recess, the children bundled up in their wraps and ran outdoors to play as usual. At the end of fifteen minutes, Miss Martin rang the bell, but they did not come in. She went to the window and looked out. She could see the school barn and the deserted house, but the storm was worse than she had thought. Through the blur of swirling snow, she could see the children's figures moving. She wondered what strange game they were playing.

Perhaps they had not heard the bell because of the wind. She went to the door and rang it again. Then, from the window, she could see them still milling around. It looked as if they did not know where they were going. She saw Delores Wagner standing under the window, close up against the building. Suddenly she realized that the little ones were lost and could not find their way to the door. They were blinded by the snow blowing in their faces.

Miss Martin ran to the front hall, took the lasso rope from the hook, opened the window and threw it out. "Delores," she shouted. "Take the rope and bring them in."

Miss Martin was not sure that Delores had heard her. She closed the window and latched it tightly. Then she watched anxiously as Delores ran out with the rope and rounded up the little children. Thinking it was a new game, each child took hold of the rope. Delores pulled them around the corner of the building and brought them in at the front door.

"Didn't you hear the bell, children?" Miss Martin called out. "I rang it twice."

"We got lost!" cried little Hulda and Peter.

"We couldn't see the schoolhouse anywhere," said the little Sticklemeyers.

There was no fear—it had all been a gay adventure. But Miss Martin's heart skipped a beat, and her face turned white.

Delores saw and understood. She knew what Miss Martin was thinking: What if it had happened while the children were walking home from school?

The older boys came tramping in.

"There's a big bunch of cattle over by the elevator," announced Darrell. "I think they're ours. We only brought one horse . . ."

"I guess we'd better go home early today, Miss Martin," said Jacob Sticklemeyer. "It's gettin' bad, so I hitched up. Buckskin's out in front with the cart."

"Yes, go right away," said Miss Martin. "Don't wait a minute."

The Sticklemeyers, big and little, bundled up and went out, calling good-by. Then in walked Oscar Meyers, the Wagners' hired man.

"Darrell, you come and help me get the cattle home," he said. "I got the truck outside."

"I just knew those cows over by the elevator were ours," said Darrell.

Konrad Snider called out, "Can I go with you, Ozzie?"

Oscar nodded. "Sure, we need all the help we can get. Come on, boys."

As they hurried to put on overshoes and sheepskins, Darrell

turned to Delores and said: "You can get home all right on Sugar, can't you?"

"Of course," said Delores. "Why not?"

As the truck drove off, Sam Englehart appeared on Silver and took Ruby up behind him. After that, the crowded schoolroom seemed empty. Only Miss Martin, the two little Hummels and Delores were left.

"Well, I guess we better start walking home," said little Peter.

"Oh *no*," said Miss Martin. "You wait here. Somebody will come for you."

"Daddy can't come." said Peter. "He went to Selfridge in the truck this morning, and said he wouldn't get back tonight."

"I think we better stay here," said Hulda. "We'll just stay all night and then we'll be here tomorrow. Daddy won't have to bring us."

"Oh, she just wants to sleep on the camp cot," explained Peter. "She never slept on a cot before."

"By golly! What a wind!" cried Delores. "Those crazy guys left the front door open."

The wind, blowing hard from the east, swept through the front hall and into the schoolroom. It sent school papers flying in every direction. Miss Martin hurried to close the front door. It opened out and she had to go outside on the porch. She tried to shut the door but couldn't. Just as she got it halfway shut, a strong gust of wind came and swung it back, almost taking her off her feet.

"Delores! Come and help!" she called.

Delores put her head out the door, and the wind almost tore her hair off. She yelled something, but Miss Martin did not hear.

"The rope!" gasped Miss Martin. "Throw me the lasso rope."

The next minute Miss Martin had the end of the rope in her hand. She tied it to the doorknob, and threw the other end back of her. "Grab it and pull," she managed to shout.

Delores stepped back inside, pulling on the rope. "Hey, you kids, come help pull the door shut!" she cried.

The rope reached into the schoolroom, and the little Hummel children pulled on it from there. They could not pull steadily, as they had to let Miss Martin step up in the doorway and get inside before the door came shut. At last the door came to, and Miss Martin latched it with a sharp blow. The children inside fell to the floor laughing, as the pull on the rope was relaxed.

"Positively no one can go out this door again tonight!" Miss Martin announced in a loud firm voice. Then she sat down on a chair, gasping for breath, and trying to fix her wind-blown hair.

The words were scarcely spoken, when the door was flung wide open again, and Pete Hummel stumbled in. Miss Martin was so

astonished, she cried out: "Man alive! What a night to be out!"

Pete Hummel shook the snow off his rubber raincoat and tight-fitting cap.

"It's not bad," he said, "only about zero."

Peter and Hulda frowned when they saw their father. They stood on the register and whispered to each other. Miss Martin knew they did not want to go home.

"You haven't come for the children, have you?" she asked. "They said you couldn't get back from Selfridge tonight. So they thought they'd just stay here."

Little Hulda sat down on the register and quickly pulled off her shoes and socks. "I got my feet wet outside at recess," she said, frowning. "I got to get my socks dry or Mama'll spank me."

She made a great fuss getting her socks dried. When she put one on, she took the other off. She never seemed to get two on at the same time.

Pete Hummel grew impatient. "That team won't stand much longer," he said.

"Didn't you come in the truck?" asked little Peter.

"No, I got the saddle horses hitched to the bobsled," said Pete. "I shouldn't be driving them, but it's hard for the larger horses to go through the snow."

"You won't take the children home in a storm like this, will you?" said Miss Martin nervously. "They'll get terribly cold, won't they?"

Pete Hummel's answer was short: "They can take it." Then he added, "I have some blankets out in the sled."

Little Peter put his sheepskin cap with fur earlaps on, then his sheepskin-lined coat and high buckle overshoes. He stood ready.

But Hulda's feet were still bare. Her father frowned at her.

"Do you want to stay here?" he asked.

"Yah," said Hulda. "It's too cold to go out."

Pete Hummel took little Peter's hand. "O. K.," he said. "We'll leave the *baby!*" They walked toward the door, where he turned and added: "No tellin' when I can come and get you. It might be a week."

"I don't care," said Hulda stubbornly. She did not mind being called a baby, or being left behind at the school. Now at last she could sleep on Teacher's cot.

The man and boy went out. Miss Martin and Delores and Hulda looked out the window. Little Peter sat up on a board placed across the one-box sled, but he was covered entirely with two blankets. He and his father slid away into the grayness of the night and the storm.

"Little Peter's trying hard to be a man," said Miss Martin softly.

"No way to know whether they'll get home safely."

Delores took Miss Martin's hand and squeezed it.

There was a great deal to do, and Delores was glad she had stayed to help. The front hall door had stood open all the time Pete Hummel was in the schoolhouse. The front hall was filled with snow which had to be swept out. The door had to be closed again, and only the lasso rope could pull it against the wind. The furnace had to be filled and coal brought up for the Heatola in the kitchen.

"Can I set up the camp cot for Hulda?" asked Delores.

"No, she can sleep with me," said Miss Martin. "Then she won't get lonely or homesick."

"Well, I guess I'll be going on home then," said Delores.

"Oh—you're not going?" cried Miss Martin. *"You* can sleep on the cot. I thought we'd eat supper first before we set it up. The kitchen is so small we can't get to the stove when the cot is up."

"Ozzie and Darrell told me to ride Sugar home," said Delores. "Mama will be looking for me. I don't want her to worry."

"Then you should have started long ago," said Miss Martin. "Do you think you can find your way all right?"

"Sugar won't let me get lost," said Delores. "She can find her way home blindfolded. I'll look for the elevator and get over to the railroad tracks, and follow the tracks all the way home." Already the girl had her snowpants, jacket and overshoes on. A twist of her scarf under her chin, a pull on her mittens, and out of the back teacherage door she slipped.

"I hate to see you go," said Miss Martin.

Delores smiled back. "It's no worse than hundreds of other times."

But before she had gone very far on Sugar's back, she knew it *was* worse. She had ridden horseback in many storms in previous years, but it had never been like this. She kept looking for the elevator, but could see it only now and then. Sugar kept her head down and did not want to hurry. Delores leaned over, patted the horse and kept talking to her.

At last, she saw the elevator close by, and was able to find the tracks. She followed the telegraph poles south and kept going. Each time when she found she had wandered off to one side, she pulled Sugar back to the flat level of the tracks again. Then she saw that the wind was covering the tracks with snow and was piling great drifts across them. The wind blew the snow in her face, so she could not see. Sugar turned around several times, and although she could see the telegraph poles, she could not tell which way she was going.

For a moment she was filled with panic. Then she spoke to herself sternly: This was the way home from school. She could walk it herself alone, at midnight, blindfolded. She knew every inch of the way. There was nothing to be frightened about. Sugar knew the way too. A horse could always find its way home by instinct, even in the worst storm. She would stop worrying and trust to Sugar.

With head bent low against the snow-laden wind, the horse plunged steadily on. Suddenly Delores noticed the wind was at her back. Had Sugar turned around and was she going back? Was she *lost?* What building was that ahead? The barn at home? The house? No—she could hardly believe her eyes. There before her was the elevator.

"Oh, you silly old Sugar!" cried the girl angrily. "What do you

mean, bringing me back here? Take me home! Take me home!"
She slapped the horse's rump sharply, and started again, following
the telegraph poles.

This time Sugar seemed more sure of herself. She walked briskly
into the wind, and kept steadily on. Delores' hands and feet grew
cold. Then the pain in her side began.

"I won't dare tell them I got lost," she whispered to herself.
"I'd never hear the end of it. Lost on the way home from school—
what a big joke! They'd think it was funny. They'd tease the life
out of me."

Delores never knew how she got home, except that Sugar took
her. After a long time, she found herself at Papa's barn. Numb
and half-frozen, she slid off the horse's back, put Sugar in the
barn and ran for the house.

"Oh, here you are at last!" cried Mama Wagner. "Why are you
so late? Why can't you start in time, when you see a storm is
coming up? Darrell said he told you to get started right after
recess. Ozzie and the boys came with the cattle long ago. They had
to follow Becklers' fence. That was the only way they could be
sure of the direction. They've gone back now to look for some of
the calves."

Mama looked sharply at Delores for the first time. The girl had
sunk down on a chair beside the stove. She was shivering with
cold. Her face was white, and she held her hand to her side.

"I ran so fast," she gasped, "I got the sideache."

"Don't you feel good?" asked Mama gently.

Sympathy was too much. Delores burst into tears. "I got lost . . .
I couldn't see where I was going . . . and Sugar started going every
which way . . ."

"Ach! Now you are safe home," soothed Mama, taking the big girl on her lap as if she were little again.

"Lost on the way home from school?" Mama could not understand. "Why, you went all the way to town in the storm in vacation, and got Christy's medicine. From school, you know the way home so well."

"I found myself back up at Oak Leaf again," sobbed Delores. "I knew I was lost when I saw the elevator. I slapped Sugar good and told her to take me home . . ." There! The whole story was out, and she hadn't intended to tell it at all.

"Sugar did," said Mama. "Sugar brought you safe home."

"My side hurts, Mama," said Delores.

"Ach! You must not run so fast," said Mama.

CHAPTER VIII

Slumber Party

"What do you think, Miss Martin," chuckled Darrell, "Delores got lost on her way home from school last Monday."

"Oh, you old tattle-tale!" Delores rushed at her brother and began to wrastle with him. He seized her by the arm, gave it a twist and made her kneel. When he let her go, she tumbled over.

"She knew she was lost when she saw the elevator!" shouted Darrell, laughing. The children laughed too.

"She started home and ended up at the elevator!" teased Emil.

"It's not funny, so there!" Delores stamped her foot angrily.

The children were back in school again, after a week's absence. Winter attendance was always so irregular, no one thought anything of it. Pete Hummel drove up in his truck, dropped his children and rode off.

"Konrad Snider's got the flu," announced Peter. "He can't come."

"I stayed by Teacher for five nights," bragged Hulda.

"Five nights?" asked Delores. "Why so long?"

Hulda shrugged her shoulders. "Nobody came for me. I slept in the *cot.*"

The Sticklemeyer cart appeared, but only Jacob and Fernetta were in it. "My brothers and sisters all got the mumps," said Fernetta with a giggle. "All but Jacob and me. We had 'em three years ago."

"I think spring's comin'," said Jacob. "Sky's so pretty and blue."

"SPRING—like fun!" laughed Darrell. "Wait till this January thaw gets over, and you'll change your mind."

"The snow's gone down a lot," said Emil Holzhauer, "on account of the warm southwest wind. That's a chinook—it always brings a thaw."

"I heard the wind whistling," said Delores, "and I came out with my snowpants on. Pop said, 'You think it's thirty below?' I was so hot, I took 'em off and left 'em home."

"There's one trouble with a thaw," said Emil. "We can't get to town because the roads are muddy and our bridge might wash out."

"We haven't been to the show since November," said Fernetta.

"I haven't been to town since Christmas," grumbled Delores. "I never get to see Katie and Norine in the winter. But I heard a bird singing on the way to school. I think it was a horned lark. Maybe winter's over. Did you wear your snowsuit?"

"Shoot, yes!" said Fernetta. "My Ma made me."

"I wanted to wear a dress this morning," said Hulda, "but Mama said it was too cold. She made me wear my jeans, one pair, not two."

Just before the last bell rang, Sam Englehart brought Ruby. She rode in a homemade box sled hitched on behind her father's horse. The children gathered round to see it.

"Silver kicks snow right in my face," complained Ruby. "Mama said it would be warmer than riding horseback, but the blankets made me hot."

"Did you bring any water, Mr. Englehart?" asked Miss Martin.

"Holy smoke!" said Sam. "I filled than ten-gallon can and came off without it. I'll bring it when I come for Ruby tonight."

"You're not coming for me, Daddy," said Ruby. "I'm staying by Teacher tonight. I brought my new blue pajamas in my over-night bag." She raised a small red suitcase, and all the children laughed.

"But Ruby . . ." Miss Martin began, "it's such a nice day . . ."

"She just wants to show off her pajamas and over-night bag she got for Christmas," said Fernetta.

"Daddy says it's going to storm," said Ruby, "so I'm staying all night."

They all looked at Sam Englehart in surprise.

"We're supposed to have a storm today," said Sam, "according to the radio. These chinooks can't be trusted, you know. Sometimes they bring the worst ones—but I sure hope it misses us." He turned to Darrell as he went out. "Keep your eye on the weather, boy. This is the worst part of the winter and a storm can come up quickly. If it looks bad, don't wait. Send the kids home in plenty of time."

The change came slowly. First the blue sky turned to a dull gray. A light drizzle began, which turned to snow in half an hour. The wind veered around to the north. The children looked up from their books restlessly. They were all weather-wise and the wind disturbed them.

"It's just a blustery wind," said Miss Martin. "It'll go down soon."

Delores looked at Darrell. They smiled. They knew more about winds than Miss Martin did. At the afternoon recess, the children came running indoors to report that it was snowing hard.

Darrell said to Delores: "Here's a nice snowstorm for you. How you gonna like riding home in this?"

"No fun," said Delores. "Wish I'd worn my snowpants."

"Gonna get lost again?" teased Darrell.

"Oh—you shut up! That's not funny," said Delores.

Work began, but Darrell was nervous. He could not settle down to his studies. A half hour passed. Then he said, "Miss Martin, I think I'd better go out and look at the weather."

"Very well, Darrell." Miss Martin respected the boy's judgment.

When he came in, his face was serious. "We all better go home quick," he said. "It's drifting already. Soon it'll be blizzarding. It's gettin' worse fast."

School broke up immediately.

"Oh dear," thought Miss Martin. "Can I get them all home— this time?" "Emil, you get your horse and go," she said. "Peter and Hulda, you wait till somebody comes for you. Jacob, go hitch up your horse. Ruby, you said you plan to stay. Darrell and Delores, you have your horses to ride."

Emil left first, before the others had their wraps on. Darrell and

Delores faced each other. It was hard to decide what to do.

"If we stay," said Delores, "we'll *be* here. Tomorrow, I mean."

"I'm going HOME," said Darrell. "We got to go quick."

"If we had a school radio, we could get the weather report and find out if it's going to be a real blizzard," said Delores.

"If we had a telephone, we could call our mothers up and ask them what to do," said Fernetta.

"I'd like to talk in one of those things," said Delores.

"Haven't you ever?" asked little Hulda Hummel.

"No, I never," said Delores.

"I have—at my Aunt Gertrude's in town," said Hulda, proudly.

"What does it sound like?" asked Delores.

"Criminy sakes!" exclaimed Darrell. "Don't stand there talkin' all day. Are you riding home or not, Delores?"

"Mama won't even be looking for us," said Delores. "She knows we've got sense enough to sleep here. She told me *never* to start out in a snowstorm again."

"You're a baby—you'll get lost!" jeered Darrell. "Lost on the way home from school!"

"That's not funny!" shouted Delores angrily. She started after her brother and began pounding his back with her fists. "Don't you dare say that again!"

Jacob Sticklemeyer came rushing in. "Come on, Fernetta. Don't be all day. Buckskin don't like to stand with the snow blowin' in his face."

"Oh, shoot!" cried Fernetta. "Wish I could stay too and have some fun. I never stayed by Teacher yet, all on account of that old Buckskin." She called good-by and ran out the door.

"Delores, you're as bad as Ruby Englehart," Darrell said angrily.

"You just want to stay. We . . . I've got to go home."

"Whatever for?" asked Delores. "We can sleep here."

"I bet our cattle are down at the haystacks," said Darrell. "I ought to be there to help go get them."

"Let Ozzie do it," said Delores. "What's a hired man for? Ozzie and Phil have brought the cattle home long ago."

"We can't pay a cent here for our food," said Darrell in a low voice. "Teacher won't take it. And we shouldn't be eating so much of her food."

"Oh, Mama sends her cream and other stuff to eat," said Delores.

"There's no feed here for the horses," said Darrell. "They can't go two days without something to eat. We can't starve our horses."

Delores was as fond of the horses as Darrell. "Maybe we can find something here for them to eat."

"And there's that sick cow," Darrell went on. "I planned to take her home tonight. I've got to do it, or she'll be dead by tomorrow."

"Oh, Darrell, just look at it!" Delores glanced out the window. "It's getting worse while we talk. You can't go out in this and chase a sick old cow home. She's probably dead already."

The boy stood still, staring out the window, watching the swirling snow in silence. Then he said slowly, "If I woulda went just when it first started blizzarding, I coulda got that cow home."

"How could you?" said Delores. "School wasn't even out yet."

"I don't want to stay," said Darrell. *"I want to go home."* There was despair in his voice. He sounded as if he were going to cry, but he didn't.

Delores came up and put her arm around his shoulder. She wanted to say, "Now, don't you cry," but she didn't, because she knew Darrell would give her a slap. "Mama'd give me heck if I let you go out in a storm like this."

"You? You let me go?" snapped Darrell. "I'm a year older'n you. I'll decide this for myself."

Delores sat down at her desk and waited. Darrell was stubborn. Nobody could push him or boss him. She covered her face with her hands, so she wouldn't see the swirling snow outside the windows. She wished there weren't so many windows—a whole row of them. It was like being out in the storm again, on Sugar, not knowing which was the way home.

Miss Martin saw Darrell standing there. She asked him if he would feed Spike and pen him in the barn for the night.

"Oh dear," thought Delores, "when he sees the horses in the barn, he'll get on Nellie and head straight for home."

Darrell was gone a long time. From the window Delores couldn't even see the barn for the snow. The wind seemed to be howling and screaming at her. It was mocking her—it was daring her to follow Darrell and go home. Should she go outside and get on Sugar's back? She sat still not knowing what to do. Teacher's alarm clock ticked off the minutes.

Then suddenly the front door banged shut, and footsteps and voices were heard in the hall. Darrell came in, with Jacob and Fernetta Sticklemeyer behind him. Delores was relieved. He hadn't gone home after all.

"Buckskin balked and wouldn't go, Miss Martin," explained Jacob. "Darrell helped me get him back in the barn. We had to put the horses in separate stalls so they won't fight. Good thing your car wasn't in the barn—we'd a had to move it out. Guess Fernetta and I will have to stay here tonight."

"I'm glad you're not going home," said Miss Martin.

Darrell cheered up, now that he had Jacob for company. A loud roar at the door and Pete Hummel came stamping in.

"Come on, kids!" he cried. "We're goin' home in the jeep."

There was no delaying this time. Hulda and Peter hurried as fast as they could, but snowpants, overshoes and coats took a long time.

"This is the second year I had my coat already, and it's gettin' too small," said Peter, "but it still keeps me warm."

"Don't you think they ought to stay, Mr. Hummel?" asked Miss Martin. "It's pretty bad out, and they're so little . . ."

"Prairie kids got to be tough," said Pete. "This weather ain't nothing." The Hummels went out and the door closed behind them.

"Miss Martin, if we stay, we want to help you," said Darrell.

"Thank you, Darrell," she replied. "Would you fix the furnace fire and get up some coal? Jacob can sweep the floor and Delores can wash the blackboards."

Delores did not move. She leaned her head on her hand. She felt tired and half-sick. Then she got up and began to erase the blackboard.

"Teacher, can Ruby and me look in your grocery box and see what you got?" asked Fernetta.

"Yes, girls," said Miss Martin. "Pick out a good supper. Let's have one mystery dish, something you never tasted before."

When Darrell came up from the cellar, his face looked serious and worried again. He brought a bucket of coal for the Heatola, but he put only a piece or two on the fire. "Miss Martin, there's not much coal left."

"I know, Darrell," she said. "I've been using as little as I can. I hope it will take us through this storm."

"Didn't Pop . . ." Darrell began, but he knew the answer to his own question.

"Papa never brought the coal!" Delores shouted angrily. "He brought coal for us and for Chris Bieber, but none for Miss Martin." Then her sudden anger turned to shame. She rushed to her desk, put her head down on her arms and sobbed. Soon the sobbing turned to coughing.

Miss Martin came over and tried to comfort her. "There's a lot of coal dust left, Delores," she said. "It makes smoke, but as long as we're warm, who cares?" She paused. "Are you taking cold?"

"I'm all right." Delores jumped up again and went to the blackboard.

In the kitchen, supper preparations had begun. The girls set out cans of tuna fish, corn, tomatoes and asparagus. Fernetta peeled potatoes and Ruby set the table. Miss Martin was sent out of the room.

"Go in and play the piano for us," suggested Fernetta.

"The piano's out of tune," laughed Miss Martin, "and half the notes don't play."

"Well, sit down and rest then," said Fernetta. "Darrell, come and stir the corn."

The little teacherage kitchen was overcrowded with cooks, as all the children helped. The calamity of the storm had turned into fun and jollity now. Delores and Jacob brought chairs, and then the door into the schoolroom was closed to keep the kitchen warm.

"Supper's ready," called Ruby.

"I'll dish out the hot stuff," said Fernetta, going to the stove. "Jeepers! Look at Darrell's corn. It smells like popcorn."

"You told me to stir it," laughed Darrell, "and I stirred it till my arm's ready to drop off."

"You popped it, you mean!" giggled Fernetta. "Hand me your plates."

"Don't give me any asper-gus," said Ruby. "I don't like it."

"*Asper-gus!* As-par-a-gus, you mean," said Delores. "That's our mystery dish. You got to eat some."

"Remember the canned *tamales* and the *tangerine* juice?" said Miss Martin. "We all tried them and liked them."

"Don't give me any," insisted Ruby. "I won't eat it."

"If you was home," said Fernetta, "your Mama'd give you a smack and you'd eat it all right."

Ruby helped herself to a big mouthful of canned corn. "Criminy sakes!" she yelled. "Darrell didn't pop it—he *burnt* it!"

The children roared with laughter, as Ruby ran to the garbage can to spit out the corn. "What a supper!" Refusing to touch

more food, she stamped into the schoolroom and sat down on the register, crying.

"Don't pay any attention to her," said Delores. "It's cold in there. She'll get over her mad pretty quick."

While Fernetta and Delores washed the dishes, Miss Martin went in to see Ruby. "What's the matter?" she asked.

"I'm cold," said Ruby, "and I'm hungry. I'm homesick too."

"If you sit on the register," said Miss Martin, "you'll get smoked up."

"It's the only warm place in the whole school," said Ruby. "I want to go home. I'm homesick for my mother. She don't make me eat burnt corn."

"If you cry," said Miss Martin, "I'm going to cry too. We'll all sit down and cry, but the storm will go on just the same. None of the children want to stay overnight. It is necessity. We may as well be cheerful and make the best of it."

Suddenly the kitchen door opened and a figure covered with a blanket rushed in. *Yi! Yi! Yi! Yi!* Loud sounds came from the figure's mouth. Loud knocks on a cardboard carton sounded somewhat like a drum. A second blanket-covered figure followed the first. An Indian dance had begun.

"Oh, you crazy boys!" Ruby had to laugh in spite of her tears.

Delores and Fernetta came out shuffling, with coats over their heads. The Indians circled faster and faster around the desks. Then Darrell tipped a desk over and fell headlong on the floor. That ended the dance.

"Let's play *New Or-leans*," said Fernetta.

Delores drew a line in chalk along the middle of the floor and they chose sides, Ruby and Miss Martin joining in. Acting out such varied actions as pitching hay and making cake, the children laughed and screamed until they were breathless.

"I'm afraid it's bedtime," said Miss Martin. "I'll see how much bedding I can scare up."

"Us boys will sleep on the floor, Miss Martin," said Jacob. "Right by the register, in the warmest spot."

"We don't need any blankets," said Darrell. "We'll sleep in our clothes."

"Here's the stage curtain, and two old coats of mine," said Miss Martin. "And how about your sheepskin coats?" Jacob brought them from the hall.

"I hope you'll be warm enough," said Miss Martin. "It's still storming out, and the furnace fire gets low by morning."

"I hope *you*'ll be warm enough, Miss Martin," said Darrell. "Don't let those fat girls in there steal all your covers. Hear them giggling?"

"Let's all settle down now," said Miss Martin, "and go to sleep."

She closed the schoolroom door and went into the bedroom. The girls insisted on nightgowns, so Miss Martin hunted out some of her own. Ruby took her new blue pajamas out of her suitcase, put them on and strutted around.

"Good night, children." Miss Martin went into the kitchen to get ready for bed. She could hear the girls giggling. Now and then Delores coughed. Suddenly Darrell's gruff voice boomed out from the schoolroom: "Shut up, you girls, us boys want to go to sleep."

"Yes, Darrie dear!" answered Delores.

The giggles became still louder, and were followed by loud whispers.

"Miss Martin, do you snore?" piped up Ruby.

"If I do," answered Miss Martin, "you call to me and I'll stop. Good night, children."

"Delores said it wasn't you snoring," Ruby continued. "It was the moaning of the wind." Giggles again.

Sleep came and brought quiet at last. The only sound was the snow-laden wind roaring around the little schoolhouse on the prairie. It was a lonesome sound and only one person heard it.

Delores lay awake worrying. Would the storm be over in the morning so they could go home? How long would the coal last? Was Mama lying awake too, worrying because they had not come? Would the night never end? Her throat felt sore and she had to cough. Suddenly she heard footsteps. She remembered the night of the prairie fire. Seeing the flare of a flashlight, she asked quickly, "Who is it?"

"I'm going down cellar to look at the furnace," said Miss Martin. "Go back to sleep. It's only three o'clock."

"Who's up? What's the matter?" Fernetta was awake too. She giggled.

"Miss Martin went down cellar," said Delores. "It's only three o'clock."

"Are you cold?" asked Miss Martin, returning. "Did I hear you cough?"

"Just my feet," said Delores. "The covers keep coming off every time Ruby rolls over." Giggles again.

"I'll heat a sad-iron for you," said Miss Martin.

Both girls were sound asleep by the time the iron got hot on the coal stove and, wrapped in a cloth, was tucked at their feet. They woke in the morning to smell the delicious aroma of coffee.

"Is it time to get up?" called Delores.

"No," said Miss Martin. "Not till the furnace gets hot." She went down cellar to put coal on.

"If you get up," called Darrell, "I'll clump you over the head with the broomstick."

The threat made Delores come out at once in her bare feet. Darrell was as good as his word. Down came the broomstick on the girl's head.

"Ouch, ouch!" she screamed, jumping back in bed.

"What's going on here?" Miss Martin was back, smiling. "Everybody getting up?"

"I hope you like this nice snowstorm of yours, Delores!" called Darrell.

"It's a present for you," answered the girl. "You can have it. What are you peeling, anyhow? Onions?"

"Yah, sure!" laughed Darrell. "Onions for your breakfast fruit."

The girls took plenty of time to get dressed. When they came out, breakfast was ready—sliced oranges, creamed salmon on toast, coffee, bread, butter and jelly. Jacob appeared, rubbing his eyes sleepily.

"I dreamed I was buried under the snow and I couldn't kick it off," he said. "How's the weather?"

"Worse and more of it," said Darrell in a disgusted tone.

"All night long the bed shook," said Ruby.

"Especially when you turned over," added Fernetta.

When the salmon was passed, Ruby turned up her nose. "I don't eat fish for breakfast," she said. "I eat *wuerst.*"

"No sausage served at this hotel," said Delores, passing her by.

Ruby changed her mind quickly. "I'm hungry, I'll eat it," she said.

As soon as he finished eating, Darrell said, "I'll take these scraps and some bread out to Spike. I want to see about the horses too. I'll get the shovel and make some paths."

Miss Martin looked out the window. It was still snowing, but the wind had died down a little. She could not see the barn at all, and all the prairie in the background was a sea of white. She watched the boy make his way through the deep snow and start shoveling paths.

"Fernetta and I·will do the dishes," said Delores. "The water pail's empty. Here, Jacob, go fill this up from the can in the front hall."

In a minute Jacob returned with an empty pail. "There's no water," he said. "Big can's empty. Cooler's empty too."

"I told you girls not to use so much water for dishes last night," scolded Ruby. "You were wasting it. You heard my father say he forgot to bring the ten-gallon can full."

Miss Martin came in. "The floor's so dirty, I want to scrub it," she said. "Did you save last night's dishwater, Delores?"

"No, I threw it out the door."

"Oh, I never do that," said Miss Martin. "I save every drop and use it over and over—for mopping the floor, cleaning overshoes, scrubbing the porch, and lots of things."

"There's not a drop of water, Miss Martin," said Delores. "We haven't washed our faces and we can't wash the dishes." She turned on Ruby. "I'd think you'd be ashamed, Ruby Englehart. It's your father's turn to bring water, and he's got a good sled to

bring it in. If he can bring *you,* there's no reason why he can't
bring us water."

The children all turned on her angrily. "He ought to forget *you*
—and bring the water!" "Jeepers! No water! Those Engleharts!"

Ruby's face turned red. "My father's no worse than yours,
Delores Wagner!" she snapped. "How about that load of COAL?"

Delores hung her head, ashamed. She could not say a word.

"I guess Darrell used the last of the water for our coffee," said
Miss Martin.

"Whatever are we gonna *do,* Miss Martin?" demanded Delores.
"We haven't even washed our faces."

"Oh, that's easy," laughed Miss Martin. "We'll melt snow for
water. I have to do it all the time. That's one thing the snow's
good for."

"Snow-water, of course," said Fernetta. "Let's all go out and
bring in snow."

"Take the lasso rope, Jacob," said Miss Martin, "and see that every one hangs onto it."

The children rushed to put on their wraps and ran outdoors. It was a great game to hold the rope. The boys shoveled snow away from the barn and the outdoor toilets. Darrell melted a pail of snow to water the horses. The girls filled Teacher's pail and dishpan with snow and set them on the stove. A kettle was filled to be used for scrubbing the floor.

"When do I get a drink?" asked Ruby.

"Not till the snow's melted, and the water's boiled, strained and cooled," said Fernetta, "unless you want to burn your throat."

Miss Martin went out on the teacherage porch. She saw the children huddled in front of the barn door. Fear clutched at her heart. Had something happened? The responsibility of keeping the children overnight or for days at a time often threw her into a panic. "What is it?" she called.

"The dog—Spike!" came the answer.

She ran out to see. Spike's head was stuck in a hole at the bottom of the door. He had dug dirt away and scratched and chewed wood off, trying to get out. The boys opened the door carefully. Freed at last, Spike ran and jumped over the snow, barking loudly.

"I'm going over to the elevator to get some oats for the horses," Darrell told Miss Martin. He started out, wading part of the way in waist-high snow, bending against the wind. Spike followed, floundering and leaping. When the boy came back, Delores saw the empty sack on his shoulder and knew he had found no grain. He said the doors were all locked.

"Where's Spike?" she asked.

"He ran off down by the stockyards," said Darrell. "I called, but he wouldn't come back. What are we going to feed the horses?"

Delores looked thoughtful. "In the early days, Grandpa said they used to stack tumbleweeds and feed them to the cattle."

"Huh!" scoffed Darrell. "Tumbleweeds under the snow, I suppose."

"There's some dry grass mixed with the coal in the cellar," said Fernetta. Fernetta ran down and brought up a few wisps, and Delores asked Miss Martin if she had any rolled oats.

"A little," said Miss Martin. "The box is only half full."

"The horses will eat it," said Delores.

"Take it then." Miss Martin smiled.

The girls took their offerings out, but the boys would not let them in the barn.

"Oatmeal!" scoffed Darrell. "Taking the last of Teacher's oatmeal. Ain't you ashamed, Delores!"

The school bell rang. Darrell gathered up the lasso rope, and they all ran in. Schoolwork began, but only one thought was uppermost: *Can we get home today?*

CHAPTER IX

A Knock at the Door

"*If we go home, we might get lost,*" said Delores.

The dreaded sentence, the basic terror was out at last. All the stories of people lost or frozen to death in snowstorms on the Great Plains, handed down over the years, rose up like ghosts in the children's memories, to frighten them.

"*We might get lost,*" Delores said again.

No one laughed. No one teased her now about getting lost on the way home from school. It was not funny any more. All morning on Tuesday, as the snow and wind increased, the children tried to forget about going home and to resign themselves to staying longer.

"Mama tells us every year not to try to go anywhere in a storm," said Delores.

"My Mama always says to go in the nearest house and wait," said Ruby.

"They can't get through to come for us," said Jacob.

"They'll come for us when they can," added Fernetta.

"They won't come at all," said Darrell angrily. "They know we've got horses. They're waiting at home for us to come. They're worrying their heads off. I think we ought to go."

"Darrell," said Miss Martin firmly. "I cannot let you start for home until the storm is over. I am responsible for all of you while you are here. It looks as if we're in for another day of it, if not more. Let's settle down and make the best of it."

"By golly! This seat's cold," complained Ruby. She slipped into Konrad Snider's seat, nearer the register. "This seat's cold, too. I bet the furnace has gone out."

"We're scraping up the coal dust to burn now," said Miss Martin. "Go put your snowpants on, Ruby. If any of you are cold, get up and run around the schoolroom until you are warm again. Or, we'll stop and play a game. I still have a couple of buckets of coal for the kitchen heater. When it gets too cold in here, we'll move to the kitchen. Let's settle down to our work now and try to forget the storm."

The children opened their books, and the room became quiet. When Delores went to the kitchen to light the kerosene stove for lunch, she looked out the north window. The storm was raging again. She could not see the elevator or the deserted house. She could not even see the school barn. The only mark in the whiteness was the faint line of telegraph poles following the railroad.

Ten-year-old Delores had seen many storms. But today she thought she had never seen such a frozen-looking world. *It must be like this at the North Pole,* she said to herself. *But nobody lives there, not even Eskimos.* The thought of the shortage of coal was a load on her heart. *If only the coal dust will last till the storm is over . . . till somebody comes . . .* She opened the teacherage door to get the food in the wooden box nailed to the outside wall, and closed it quickly.

"Everything in your icebox is frozen solid, Miss Martin," she called. "The cream and the smearcase and everything. We forgot to bring them in."

Miss Martin went on correcting papers at her desk. "Find some cans of soup to warm up," she said. "We need something hot."

"The cocoa box is empty, Miss Martin."

"There's some tea left, I think."

Suddenly Delores heard a sound and looked out. "The Galloping Goose!" she cried. "There's the train!"

The children dropped their work and came running. They crowded into kitchen and bedroom and looked out across the whitened prairie. They saw a vague form moving slowly beneath the line of telegraph poles.

"It's the snowplow," said Darrell. "Engine, caboose and snowplow."

"A steam engine," said Jacob. "That pretty little Diesel couldn't buck drifts like this."

"There hasn't been a train for days now," said Miss Martin. "I'm surprised they are keeping the branch line open."

"They're just trying to," said Darrell. "That snowplow will soon back up and return to town, I bet."

After lunch, when Delores and Fernetta were washing the dishes, they heard a curious scratching. They looked at each other, startled. They could hear it plainly above the roar of the wind, close at hand.

"A mouse!" cried Fernetta.

"No," said Delores. "It sounds like a dog scratching on the door. I bet it's Spike. He's come back and wants in." She opened the teacherage door a crack, and Spike put his nose in.

"Poor thing," said Fernetta. "He's half frozen. Let him come in by the stove."

But Spike did not want to come in or lie down. He whined and started running back down the steps. "Golly! Shut the door quick!" cried Ruby.

"Something's wrong," said Darrell. "I'm going to follow him and see what he wants."

"It's not safe for you to go out, Darrell," said Miss Martin. "Bring Spike inside. He's cold and hungry." Darrell pulled the dog in.

Fernetta opened a can of prepared macaroni, and the dog gulped it greedily. He lay down in front of the Heatola, but seemed restless. Now and then he got up, went to the teacherage door and whined.

"Something's wrong," said Darrell again. "Spike's acting strange."

The boy tried to study, but was disturbed. The children went on with their lessons, but the storm kept on getting worse. The wind seemed to be blowing against every window.

Suddenly a knock came at the door. It was a sharp, insistent, purposeful knock. It startled the children—they jumped. They looked at each other and at Miss Martin. Spike jumped up and barked loudly. Who could it be, way off in this isolated place, with no one around for miles?

"Lie down, Spike!" scolded Darrell. "Be a good dog."

"Go to the door, Darrell," said Miss Martin.

Darrell opened the teacherage door and some one almost fell in. It was a young boy, about eight years old, covered with snow. Darrell took him by the arm and led him to a chair. He sat down, gasping for breath, and rested. The children huddled together, staring at him. He was an Indian boy, dressed in heavy winter clothes. His face looked pale and pinched. No one recognized him. He pointed out the door.

"Somebody's in trouble out there," said Darrell. "I'm going out to see who it is. Spike will show me where to go." He looked at Miss Martin defiantly. She said nothing. Hastily he put on his wraps and overshoes, and went out the door with Spike ahead of him.

"I'm going with Darrell," said Delores at once. "He mustn't go alone."

"Oh *no!*" cried Miss Martin. "Not with your sore throat and cough. I can't let you."

"I'll go with him," said Jacob. He had his wraps already on.

"Take the lasso rope and stay together," said Miss Martin.

Rope in hand, Jacob followed Darrell out through the snowstorm.

Miss Martin and the girls looked after the Indian boy. Delores brought a panful of snow and bathed his frozen hands and feet. Fernetta warmed up soup and Miss Martin fed him. Ruby straightened Miss Martin's bed and they led him in. He lay down and fell asleep at once.

It seemed a long time before the two boys came back. Spike

bounced up on the porch, barking, and in came the two boys leading an Indian woman with a tiny baby in her arms. She, too, was half-frozen, and needed warmth and food. She smiled, but could not speak.

"She was waiting under the loading chute of the stockyard," said Darrell. "That's where Spike went, when he left me this morning—I bet they were there then. The chute was a little protection from the storm. Waiting for the train, she said. That's all we could get out of her."

"If she'd gone in the depot, it would have been better," said Jacob. "She could have closed the door and kept the wind out."

"Why, there's a stove in the depot," said Delores. "The section men build a fire there and hang their wet gloves up on those bent wires to dry. She could have had a fire."

"Indian women don't carry matches," said Ruby.

"The coal's locked up in the storage half of the depot," said Jacob.

School work was forgotten in the emergency. Miss Martin and the children tried to think of ways to help the Indian woman. She ate and fed the baby soup but refused to go to bed. She sat stolidly in a chair by the Heatola, waiting patiently for her son to wake up.

"The train, the train," she kept saying.

"I bet she thought that snowplow going north was a passenger train, and would soon be coming back," said Jacob.

"I bet she wants to go to town," said Fernetta. "Man alive! What a trip—on foot, without even a horse! Do you suppose they walked here?"

"I know who she is now," said Darrell. "She's Charlie Spotted Bear's wife. They live on Oak Creek, up toward Fort Yates. Pop leases their land. They must have walked all the way down here to get the train."

"I recognize her now," said Delores. "They're always going through our place on their way to Bullhead—in their wagon in the summertime. Mama always gives them something to eat. They never come in winter, though."

"Pearl Spotted Bear, yes!" The Indian woman smiled. "Bullhead, train."

"She's on her way to Bullhead," said Delores. She turned to the woman and explained: "No trains, big storm, no trains."

"Going to Bullhead in a storm like this," said Miss Martin. "No trains for the past two weeks, and no signs of let-up in the storm. Well, at least we have food here, and we'll try to keep warm. Boys, we'll let the furnace fire go out now, and burn what coal and dust we have left in the kitchen heater. We can all crowd into the kitchen and bedroom, I think."

"Let's bring our books and papers out by the stove," said Ruby.

After sleeping an hour, the Indian boy woke up. He smiled happily to see his mother and baby sister safe in the kitchen. Rested and warmed through, he began to talk.

"Big, big snow. It's sure cold, this morning the zero is forty below. Much cold weather keeps people healthy yet." He smiled hopefully, and no one laughed. He accepted cold weather as an inevitable thing, which one could not escape, but had to endure.

"Spike, our dog, he found you," said Darrell.

"Big dog bite," said the Indian boy. "We 'fraid."

"Spike only wanted to help you," said Darrell.

"Pretty soon old train come, we go Bullhead," said the boy.

"No trains running," said Darrell, shaking his head. "You stay here."

"We pretty near froze up, we sleep in big snow." The boy smiled as if he were joking, then his face turned sad, with all the tragic sadness of his race.

"You would have frozen sure," said Darrell. "Spike saved you."

"I could have told them the best way to keep from freezing is to wiggle like a worm," said Jacob. The children laughed.

"They can sleep here," said Miss Martin. "We'll find a way to make them comfortable."

"Us girls will give them our bed and sleep on the floor," said Delores.

"Sure mike!" exclaimed Fernetta. "We're as tough as the boys. We can sleep on the floor if the boys can."

"The floor's plenty hard," laughed Jacob.

"Especially toward morning," added Darrell.

"What do we care!" cried Delores.

"I just wish I had more bedding," said Miss Martin.

Ruby stood still, frowning. Suddenly she burst out: "They're Indians. They're used to sleeping on the floor. Why do we have to give them our bed?"

"Because we *want* to," said Fernetta.

"What do you think, children?" asked Miss Martin.

All spoke but Ruby: "They should have a good bed to sleep in."

Fernetta turned on Ruby. "You dumb-bell, can't you see they're half dead? If you'd walked ten miles in a storm and waited half-a-day in a snowbank, wouldn't a bed feel good to you? Can't you even feel sorry for them?"

"Maybe my Daddy will come for me before night," said Ruby. "Then I won't have to sleep on the floor."

"Oh *you!*" scolded Delores. "All you think about is yourself."

Suddenly a loud roaring was heard above the storm.

"The train! The Galloping Goose!" cried the children. "The snowplow must be coming back," shouted the boys.

The roaring sound grew louder, louder than any train. The Indian woman rose quickly from her chair, bundled her baby up and rushed out the door, pulling the boy behind her.

"Oh *no!*" cried Miss Martin. "You must not go. You can't get over to the depot in time. The train will be gone. The snowplow won't take passengers, I'm sure."

But there was no holding the Indian woman and boy. Down the teacherage steps they went, out into the storm.

"There's no train. That wasn't a train at all," cried the children, looking out the kitchen window. "I bet it's a tractor." They ran out on the little back porch. Now the roaring sound became louder.

"It's an airplane!" shouted the boys. "It's circling around over the schoolhouse. It's coming nearer. It's trying to land."

Through the falling flakes, the form of a Piper Cub airplane could be distinctly seen. The Indian family was quickly forgotten in view of this new excitement. The boys ran in the snow, pointing upwards.

"I bet it's Peter Hummel's uncle," shouted Darrell. "He brought Peter's father and mother and circled the schoolhouse once last year, but couldn't land because of the drifts."

"Whoever it is, this fellow's gettin' ready to land," said Jacob.

"There's three things I never rode in," said Ruby, "a train, an airplane and a boat."

"Miss Martin, does it look like Paul Kruger's plane?" asked Delores.

"I can't see for the snow," said Miss Martin nervously. "I wonder what a plane would be coming here for . . ."

Teacher and children stood tense and silent close to the schoolhouse, without coats or wraps, unmindful of cold and snow, watching the plane. Beside the school barn, the Indian woman and boy waited and watched too. The plane came slowly down, landing in the open windswept stretch between barn and schoolhouse. It came slowly to a dead stop. The engine purred a while, then died away.

"It's got skis on it!" yelled the boys. Jacob and Darrell ran over at once. The door opened and out stepped Paul Kruger.

"Paul!" cried Miss Martin. "It's Paul Kruger." She rushed up to greet him.

"You all right . . . ?" asked Paul. His voice was tense and his face looked haggard and tired. "You and the children?"

"Yes, we're all right," said Miss Martin. She burst into tears and had to hide her face in her hands. "How did you know, Paul?"

"When I heard you had no coal," Paul Kruger began, "I was mad as an old setting hen. I loaded up at once . . ."

"You've brought us COAL?" Miss Martin smiled. "Who told you?"

"Gustaf Wagner said his brother never got any hauled out to you before the storm. Everybody's worried about Oak Leaf School. They told about you on the radio—marooned with a lot of children and no coal."

"And we thought we were completely forgotten," said Miss Martin. "Oh Paul! Did you remember that other winter so long ago, when you were about ten years old, and we ran out of coal?"

"I sure do," said Paul, "and there weren't any airplanes then. Here's your mail and newspapers." He tossed a bumpy feedsack into Miss Martin's arms. "You might like to read about this record-breaking storm you've been living through—worst one in fifty years, they say."

"Thank you, Paul," said Miss Martin. "For weeks I've had no mail, not a word from Aunt Molly . . ."

"Boys, help me unload this coal quick," said Paul. "It will be enough to last till they can get a truckload through. I've got to rush back to town. Everybody needs help—sick babies, people needing operations and waiting to be flown to the doctor, cows without hay. I'm worn out—can't even stop to talk."

Soon the boys were emptying coal out of sacks through the cellar window. The sound of falling coal was a welcome one.

"I brought groceries too," said Paul. "Your car—where is it?"

"There," said Miss Martin, pointing. "You can just see the top.

It's buried in that big drift."

"Will it run?" asked Paul. "You got No-Freeze in the radiator?"

Miss Martin nodded, as the girls carried paper bags full of groceries into the kitchen.

"Yippee!" cried Ruby. "Now I'll eat again. I'm tired of starving . . ."

"Starving?" cried Delores. "What do you mean?"

Paul waited while the boys shoveled and swept the snow off Miss Martin's car. Darrell brought the car key and Paul soon had the engine going. "Your car's O. K.," he said. "Plenty of gas in the tank too. That's good."

"Paul, just one more thing before you go." Miss Martin pointed to the little Indian family, still standing by the barn. She told their story.

"I'll fly them back to town with me," said Paul, "where they can find shelter and food. They can get to Bullhead from there as soon as the roads are opened up."

When the Piper Cub plane took off, it was minus a load of coal and two weeks' supply of groceries, but it carried an Indian boy, woman and baby. The children waved happily as they watched the plane rise in the air and disappear from sight.

School life seemed a little tame to come back to, afterwards. But the best part about it was the heat in the schoolroom. The boys fairly fought for a chance to shovel coal on the furnace.

"It's not snowing so much now, Miss Martin," said Darrell. "But I s'pose you won't let us go home tonight."

"How can I, Darrell," answered Miss Martin, "after what Paul Kruger told me? It's the worst storm in fifty years, coming so soon after last week's snow—and it's not over yet. All the roads in Cor-

son County are blocked, no trains running, no cars, trucks, jeeps
—only planes. Perhaps by tomorrow . . . but we'll have to wait
and see what tomorrow brings."

"Then we've got to sleep here again tonight," growled Darrell.

"I'm afraid so."

"I just wish I knew what's happened to our cattle," the boy burst
out. "I bet they're all buried deep in snow."

"Worrying won't help them, Darrell," said Miss Martin.

"And our horses here," the boy went on. "This is their second
day with nothing to eat. If I'da let them out on the range yesterday, they woulda rustled their own food. Horses can paw the snow
away and get grass."

"This snow's too deep," said Delores, "and saddle horses are
not much good at rustling, you know that. Maybe we can find
them something . . ."

"Oh—you and your Rolled Oats!" snapped Darrell.

"I know what!" cried Fernetta, with a giggle. "Let's feed them
the Christmas tree."

"Jeepers!" cried Delores. "Why didn't we think of that before?
Sugar will eat it, I bet. I saw her nibbling it once when I had her
tied there by the steps."

Miss Martin had stuck the school tree into a large snowdrift
beside the teacherage steps, when she returned after Christmas vacation. She liked to tie scraps of fat and suet to its branches to
attract the winter birds. The tree relieved the bleakness of the view
from the back door and gave her a measure of comfort. She hated
to see the tree go, but if the horses were hungry enough to eat it,
how could she deprive them of a meal?

She said nothing. The girls pulled the Christmas tree out of the snowbank and Delores carried it to the barn. In a short time they came back and put the tree, somewhat the worse for wear, in its former place.

"The crazy old horses thrashed it around and tramped it," said Fernetta, "but they never took a bite."

"Guess they're not very hungry," said Ruby. "Guess they're not half as starved as I am."

But the children were used to Ruby's complaining by now, and paid no attention to it.

"I bet the horses are thirsty," said Delores. She brought in a dishpan of snow-water and melted it for them.

"They don't want water either," she said when she came back from the barn. "They just want to go home."

"So do I," said Ruby.

CHAPTER X

Sick of School

The second night at the schoolhouse wasn't half as much fun as the first. The fact that the storm continued made the children fearful and anxious. They were all tired and ready to go to bed early. Miss Martin assembled coats for the boys to sleep on, and set up the camp cot.

"Oh look, Miss Martin!" cried Ruby, coming out of the bedroom in her blue pajamas. "The stovepipe's red hot."

"We can't have that," answered Miss Martin.

"Somebody put on too much coal," scolded Ruby.

"It might set the chimney on fire," said Darrell. He quickly

133

opened the front stove door, to cool the fire off.

"I'll have to sit up and watch it," said Miss Martin.

After the girls had stopped giggling, and Jacob had gone to sleep, Darrell came out in the kitchen. "I'll watch the stove too, Miss Martin," he said. "I can't sleep. That new coal sure does burn hot."

"When this heater gets red hot," said Miss Martin, "it just refuses to be shut off. It keeps on burning furiously."

"What were you thinking about, sitting here by yourself?" asked the boy.

"I was wondering where we would go if the building caught on fire," said Miss Martin. "These Dakota schoolhouses often catch fire from overheated stoves. Perhaps I was borrowing trouble."

"We could go to the Swartz's house," said Darrell. "That's the nearest place, but it's not much in the way of shelter."

"It must be filled with snow, now that the windows are broken," said Miss Martin, "but I think there's a range in the old kitchen."

"The Oak Leaf depot would be better," said Darrell. "There's a good stove and the section men usually leave some kindling. They keep the coal locked up in the storage half. But it would be dry in the waiting room and sheltered from the wind. We'd have to take some matches in our pockets."

"It's strange the Indian woman didn't go in there," said Miss Martin.

"The door was shut tight," said Darrell. "She probably thought it was locked, and never even tried it. Good old Spike—he rescued that Indian family, didn't he? If it hadn't been for Spike, they'd have frozen to death."

He patted the dog, now stretched out at his feet. The two sat quietly, watching the red glow of the stovepipe grow pale.

"It's twelve o'clock, Darrell," said Miss Martin. "We'd better both turn in. We'll need our strength . . . for what's ahead tomorrow."

In spite of his late bedtime, Darrell was the first one up.

"Man alive! What a storm!" he cried, staring out the window. "Is it never going to stop? Are we going to have to stay here forever? This is Wednesday, isn't it?"

"Yes," said Miss Martin, "I'm thankful morning has come, and every one is safe. Delores has a cold—that is all. Hurry and dress, girls, while I'm tending the furnace. I can't reach the stove to get breakfast until the cot is folded and put away."

"Hey, Delores!" called Darrell. "Come look at this awful snowstorm of yours."

"Golly, what a dinky little kitchen," complained Ruby. "Six people cooking and eating here, stepping on each other's toes and bumping into each other."

Nobody spoke of going home. One glance out the window was enough. All morning the wind blew and the snow piled up higher and higher. Soon Miss Martin's car was buried again, deep in a huge drift. Schoolwork moved half-heartedly, as the endless day dragged on.

At noon, every one seemed cross. Miss Martin was too tired to cheer the children up. Nerves grew tense, and bickering began. Fernetta Sticklemeyer bumped into Ruby Englehart and spilled the baked beans on the floor. She had to let Spike eat them up, and open two more cans. Ruby sat by the register and sulked. She refused to set the table or to help in any way.

"I have to do housework at home," explained Ruby. "Why

should I do it at school too? I came here to visit. My Mama says I don't have to work."

"Them that don't work can't eat," snapped Fernetta.

"You just better give me something to eat, Fernetta Stickle-meyer," began Ruby angrily, "or I'll . . ."

"Now, children," said Miss Martin. "Let's not quarrel and make things worse than they are. There's plenty of food for everybody."

"I'm tired of staying here," Ruby went on. "I'm sick of school."

"We're all sick of school," said Delores. "Miss Martin's sick of school too. She'd like to go and visit her aunt in Aberdeen."

"I'm sick of this mean old snowstorm," said Darrell.

"I'm sick of school, I said," insisted Ruby. "I'm going home today."

"How you gonna get there?" asked Jacob.

"Walk!" said Ruby. "I got two good long legs."

"Long legs!" repeated Fernetta. "I'll say she has—she can run like a rooster!"

"But she's as sour as a pickle," said Delores. The children laughed.

"If nobody comes for me today," Ruby went on, "I'm gonna walk home."

"O. K. Go ahead," jeered Jacob. "Go pack your over-night bag. Better start now, if you want to get there before midnight. Three miles and half is a long way to go in deep snow like this."

"Tell us when to come and dig you out of the snowbank," said Darrell.

"Leave your two good long legs stickin' out, so we can see 'em," said Delores. The children laughed, but Ruby did not.

When Fernetta dished the beans out, Darrell took a large bite and cried out: "Criminy! I burned a green streak all the way to my stomach!"

The children laughed again.

"What's the matter, Delores? You're not eating," said Fernetta. "You gettin' fussy like Ruby? I thought you liked beans."

"I'm not hungry," said Delores. "I can't eat today."

"I'll feed you!" cried Darrell. He took a large spoonful of beans and tried to poke them down his sister's throat.

"Darrie, *don't!* You're crazier than a pet coon," said Delores. "Let me *alone!*" She went into the bedroom, coughing badly.

Miss Martin followed her, and soon came out again. "Delores' throat looks bad," she said, "and I don't like that cough of hers. We'll be quiet and let her sleep awhile."

"Man alive!" laughed Darrell. "There's nothing the matter with her. She's just playin' possum. That girl's tough—a little snow-storm like this wouldn't get *her* down."

But under his words of bravado, Miss Martin knew the boy was worried.

"Is nobody coming?" The children kept asking the same question over and over all afternoon. The snow had stopped now and the wind had gone down, but the thermometer registered 5° below zero.

"What's the matter with their jeeps and tractors?" asked Darrell.

"Why don't they get out and shovel?" said Jacob.

But all questions remained unanswered. The world outside the schoolhouse was white and silent. Now that the storm had died down, it was so white and silent, it seemed as if life itself had left it.

"The winter birds and the field mice must be buried deep in the snow," said Darrell. "I haven't seen a bird anywhere."

"Not a bird has come to feed at the Christmas tree since the storm began," said Miss Martin.

When the afternoon work was done, the children begged to go outside. They shoveled paths to the barn and opened the doors. They found the horses nervous and fractious, anxious to be out again. The boys got on their backs and rode them out, but the drifts were so high, they could not go far and were soon glad to come back to the barn.

"Jeepers! It's pretty out," said Ruby, standing at the window, pointing to the drifts. "The snow looks just like Mama's seven-minute cake frosting."

"You're crazy," said Fernetta. "The drifts look like cliffs in the Bad Lands. Some are like wings with pretty feather designs, some are like boats sticking up, and some are like winding tunnels."

The boys came running in, excited. "There's a big flock of pheasants out by the barn. Got anything to feed them?"

"A new box of Rolled Oats that Paul Kruger brought," said Miss Martin. "Will that do?"

The boys took it and ran. Tamed by hunger, the beautiful birds came close to get food. Their bronze and brightly colored feathers stood out brilliantly against the snow. They pecked hungrily at the oats.

The third day passed and another night came. About noon on Thursday, the fourth day, the children heard the welcome sound of a roaring motor. They stood still and looked at each other. The roaring seemed to echo and re-echo over the silent snowbound prairie. It was music to their ears.

"A jeep!" "A tractor!" they shouted. "Someone is coming!"

Filled with excitement, they ran outside and waited to see who it was. Delores woke up from a feverish nap and came to look out the window, with Miss Martin beside her. The roaring came closer and closer. After a long time, a tractor came crawling over the brow of the hill, where the snow had blown thinnest.

"It's Pop!" cried Jacob and Fernetta. *"It's Pop come to take us home!"* The happy words were like a little song: *It's Pop come to take us home.*

Darrell and Ruby begged to be taken along, but Al Sticklemeyer shook his head. "You live in the wrong direction, Darrell," he said. "I can take Ruby—she can sleep at our house till her folks can get over. Her Dad's likely to be over tomorrow to get me to help him open our road."

"Ruby, do you want to go to the Sticklemeyers?" asked Miss Martin. "Or do you want to stay here?"

"I'm sick of school," said Ruby. "I'll go anywhere to get away."

"You'll have to sleep in a bed with my three little sisters," warned Fernetta.

"I don't care," said Ruby. "Maybe I'll get something decent to eat."

"Sauerkraut!" warned Delores, laughing.

"We'll leave the cart here," said Al Sticklemeyer. "Jacob, you hang onto Buckskin's bridle and let him walk behind. We got to go slow to get around the drifts."

As the tractor crept slowly over the hill, the figures of three children standing beside the driver made a dark silhouette against the sky. Ruby lifted her over-night bag and waved it.

"Out of the frying-pan into the fire!" cried Darrell in a mocking voice. "That'll be good for Ruby—the Sticklemeyers stepping all over her in that little three-room house."

"Oh, I forgot!" exclaimed Miss Martin. "They've got the *mumps!*"

"Don't worry," said Delores. "She's had 'em."

"Too bad!" laughed Darrell.

The schoolhouse seemed quiet now, with only Darrell and Delores there, but Darrell knew that Miss Martin was relieved. He could see by this time, too, that Delores was sick, so he said nothing about going home. But in his heart, he was overcome with anxiety because of the necessity for the prolonged stay. He felt hopeless, too, when he saw more snow coming down. Would the storm never end? Delores went back to bed, saying she did not want to eat, and Darrell helped to set out the supper. He lighted the lamp when it was nearly dark. As he and Miss Martin were eating, they heard once again the heavy roar of a motor.

"Well, I'll be jiggered!" Darrell jumped up and ran out.

"It's a snowplow!" the boy yelled, jumping up and down. "It's Pop and Ozzie with the tractor and road-clearing outfit. Jeepers! It's Pop come at last. Hey, Delores, we can go home! Oh, Pop, where the heck you been this long time? We thought you would never get here."

But Johannes Wagner's ears were deafened by the motor and he did not hear. He made a road around the schoolhouse and to the school barn, pushing a mountain ridge of snow off onto the edge of the prairie.

Miss Martin quickly put a pot of coffee on the stove and had it ready when Johannes came stumbling in. Ozzie stayed outside, turning the plow around. Johannes wore a smile from ear to ear, in spite of the sub-zero night. He was bundled in many layers of clothes and covered with snow. Icicles clinging to his eyebrows and whiskers had to be melted off before he could speak, eat or drink his coffee.

"Nice little storm we been havin'," he said with a grin.

"Oh Pop!" cried Delores. She felt better at once, and had jumped out of bed. "We thought you would never come. Seems like we been stayin' here forever." She went to the front hall, got her wraps and began to put them on.

Mr. Wagner turned to Miss Martin: "You got the coal? Paul Kruger got through all right?"

"Yes," said Miss Martin. "We were down to the last bucketful . . . and there were six of us, besides an Indian family of three . . ."

"I could kick myself for lettin' it go so long," said Johannes. "After all you done for our kids . . . I kept puttin' it off too long—never thought we'd get this big storm on top of the others. Minna's been cryin' her eyes out thinkin' of you here all alone with no one but these kids."

"They've been a wonderful help to me," said Miss Martin.

"Oh Pop," cried Delores, "let's go home quick. My throat's sore and—"

"I got to be rolling along," said Johannes. "Got to get a load of hay for the cattle tonight."

"Are the cattle all right?" asked Darrell anxiously. "Where are they? You got to get hay *tonight?*"

"It's already loaded," said Johannes, "but I got to start the truck to haul it to them. If the truck won't start, I'll have to build a fire under it. Or else—drive the cattle home."

"Oh Pop, I want to go with you," begged Delores.

"Got to catch Queen too," Johannes went on. "We been havin' all kinds o' trouble. Ozzie rode Queen over to Arlo Beckler's yesterday, but the drifts were so deep, he had to get off and walk. He turned Queen loose to come home, but she didn't come. She's somewhere out on the prairie with my best saddle on her back. Phil tried to find her but couldn't."

"Oh Pop . . ."

Johannes looked hard at Delores. "Listen, girl, it's still snow-ing," he said. "I ain't been home for two days and two nights, ain't had a wink o' sleep all that time. Been tryin' to get some roads open. People are hungry, they can't get food. We got to open the roads. Your Mama's worryin' her head off. She thinks I'm buried deep in snow. No tellin' when I'll get home, with more snow comin' down . . ."

"We thought it was funny you didn't come for us," said Darrell, "but I can see the reason why, now."

"I got to be rolling along," said Johannes. He gulped down another cup of hot coffee, and poured a cup to take out to Ozzie.

"I can drive the cattle to the hayrack," said Darrell. He had his wraps and overshoes on, and was ready to start. "What about the horses here, Pop? They ain't had a bite to eat for four days."

"Turn 'em loose," said Johannes. "They'll come home and we'll feed 'em. You stay here, Delores. I can't take two on the tractor."

"Oh Pop!" cried Delores. *"I want to go home."*

"Delores doesn't feel well . . ." began Miss Martin.

"It may be *hours* before I reach home," said Johannes. "You better stay here, girl, and keep warm." He grinned. "At least now you've got coal and have heat. Got stuff to eat?"

"Yes—plenty," said Miss Martin.

"Oh Pop . . ." Delores felt like crying, but didn't. "You gonna turn Sugar loose? How'll I get home without a horse to ride?"

"We'll come and get you soon as we can," said Johannes. He and Darrell went out the door and down the teacherage steps. Later, Darrell ran back with Ozzie's empty coffee cup. He called good-by, but Delores did not answer.

She sank down on a kitchen chair, tired, sick and disappointed. After resting a minute, she took off her wraps, went to the front hall and hung them up neatly. She took her overshoes off and came back to the kitchen. She ate a little soup, then sat by the table, while Miss Martin read her letters and newspapers by lamplight. Miss Martin spoke of good news from her aunt in Aberdeen, then talked about the latest storm news.

"All the roads are blocked," she said, "and so many people have been stalled in cars. It says here, when you go anywhere in a car, to always carry ashes, a shovel and a tow rope with you; to wear heavy clothing and carry blankets along. 'Don't keep the engine going when you get stalled. Be sure to keep one window open slightly.'"

"Your car's covered so deep with snow," said Delores. "I don't guess we'll be goin' anywhere. We'll just stay here."

"I'm glad I bought that lasso rope," said Miss Martin, remembering how useful it had been.

"Those little Sticklemeyers were going every which way," laughed Delores, "till I went out and corralled them in. And we never woulda got that front door shut in that east wind, without it."

"The newspaper tells how to signal for airplanes, too," said Miss Martin.

"I heard that on the radio at home," said Delores, "before the battery went dead. Make the letter L if you need fuel or oil. F for food and water. I forget what the others were."

"It says here: 'A straight line ten feet long, for serious injury, or to call a doctor. Two L's side by side mean *all's well.* If in doubt, make SOS.' That's the international distress signal."

"Mama said it sounded like nonsense to her," said Delores. "The wind would blow snow over the marks. The airplane pilot couldn't see a thing."

"It says 'ashes can be used, if there is no wind,' " Miss Martin went on. " 'Otherwise use strips of fabric, pieces of wood, stones or any available material. Or, if the wind is not blowing, signals can be made by dragging, shoveling or tramping the snow.' " She paused and smiled. "We didn't have to signal our plane to come, did we?"

"Paul Kruger seemed to know we needed him," said Delores.

"He was like that as a boy," said Miss Martin. "Always thoughtful, anticipating my needs. No wonder he turned into a 'mercy flyer.' "

"I didn't get to ask Pop how Mama is . . . and Christy," said Delores. "It seems a month since I saw them."

"They are safe at home, so don't worry," said Miss Martin. "The main thing now is to doctor you up and get rid of that cold of yours. Then, when they come for you, you'll be ready to go home."

"When Papa gets home," laughed Delores, "Mama's sure to send him right back to get me."

"Of course," said Miss Martin.

"I'm glad I didn't go out tonight," said Delores. "I feel too sick. Bed's the place for me."

CHAPTER XI

Rough Going

It was a good thing Delores did not try to go home. All Thursday night she was very ill. She felt sick to the stomach and had sharp pains in her side. She vomited often. Neither she nor Miss Martin slept. Miss Martin never undressed at all. She sat on a chair beside the bed where the girl lay. When morning came, the sky was clear and the pink and golden sunrise across the white snowdrifts was dazzling. A strong gale was blowing.

Miss Martin went down cellar to take care of the furnace. While she was getting breakfast, there came a grinding sound, then a loud crash.

"Oh!" Delores jumped. "What was that?"

"My ice-boxes," said Miss Martin. "The boxes nailed on the wall outside. They're rolling across the prairie now."

"The wind will pick the schoolhouse up next," said Delores, "and roll it around like a giant tumbleweed."

After a while, another bang came, this time from the front hall.

"Bricks falling off the chimney," said Miss Martin. "The mortar's loose. Too bad they don't keep up the repairs on this building. It was a good building when it was new, in 1920. It's only thirty years old."

"Pop says they won't use it much longer," said Delores. "They'll try to haul us to town by bus, I suppose."

"In snowstorms like this?" Miss Martin laughed.

Delores had no appetite, but Miss Martin ate a bowl of cereal. Then she shoveled the snow from the front porch and hall. "It's plenty cold, a little above zero," she said when she came back in. "There hasn't been so much snow inside the front door any winter since I began teaching here. I'm going to sweep the snow out of my car, and off the top, then see if the engine will start."

"Do you think it will?" asked Delores.

"Yes," smiled Miss Martin. "It has surprised me lots of times. Darrell had it going on Tuesday. I'd better try it again—don't know when I may need it." She looked hard at Delores. "You're feeling a little better, aren't you?"

"My side hurts bad when I cough," said Delores, trying to be hopeful. She did not want to worry Miss Martin. "Is appendicitis on the right or the left side?"

But Miss Martin was already out the door. "You stay in bed and keep warm," she called back.

Suddenly a loud crash was heard, followed by the clatter of broken glass. "Oh!" cried Miss Martin from the porch. "The car windows!"

She looked down and saw that one of the large east storm windows had come off. It was teetering on the car's fender. Somehow it had missed hitting the windows. "I'll have to see if I can lift it off and lay it on the snowbank."

"Everything that's loose around this old school has been blown off by this time," said Delores grimly.

The car was as completely covered with snow as if the boys had never cleared it off. Miss Martin shoveled and swept until she was tired. She started the engine and while it was running, put the chains on. While she worked, panting from exertion, she tried to decide what she should do.

She knew that Delores was seriously ill and in need of a doctor. Should she try to get her home to her parents? Would they realize how sick she was—that it was appendicitis, and not just a cold? If it was appendicitis, no time should be wasted in getting her to a doctor, but should this be a teacher's responsibility?

What to do? No telephone and the snow so deep. Even with clear weather, the thermometer could not seem to rise above zero. Whatever was to be done would have to be done in this freezing cold. The actual storm was over. If that cold wind would die down, it wouldn't be too bad out. Could she drive the car anywhere?

Then she thought, "If I can't drive, I can still walk."

Should she walk somewhere for help? Some drifts would hold a person up, others would let you sink with a jolt. That kind of walking was slow and exhausting. It would mean leaving the sick girl alone for long hours.

Why did no one come? Was she cut off from all living creatures? Was she entirely alone in this isolated place? She knew she was not, that her strength came from a Higher Power. If only Paul had come a few days later with his plane. . . . But the coal had been a godsend these last three days. Should she signal him and wait, in the vain hope that he might be flying in this direction again? No— he would not be back. He was needed elsewhere.

Then Miss Martin remembered the Galloping Goose. The engine with snowplow and caboose had gone north the day that Paul came, and had never returned south. She had often caught the Goose to go to town. If it went up one day, it would come down the next day at a quarter to twelve. Sometimes it was as late as three, and once when the weather was bad, it was as late as six. But it always came down sooner or later. She thought of the old saying: *What goes up must come down!* and smiled to herself. It was a comforting thought.

"There's the depot—we can wait there." Like a ray of light in a dark place, the solution presented itself. "I'll take coal for the stove, and we will wait there until it comes. There's a telephone too. . . . If I can get it to work, I can ask for help." Any kind of action was better than waiting. She'd try it anyhow. Renewed strength came to give her courage.

"I'm going to take you to town to the doctor," she told Delores, when she went in.

Delores smiled. She was too sick now to realize what that simple sentence meant. Gripped by pain, her only thought was a hope for relief.

"I have no skirt," she said. "I always wear a skirt when I go to town."

"I'll give you one of mine to wear over your jeans," said Miss Martin. "Put this sweater on under your coat. I'll buckle up your overshoes, and I'll take my grandmother's homespun blanket along. That will keep you warm."

Miss Martin made her preparations carefully. She put two buckets of ashes in the car, a large box of coal, a shovel, and several blankets. Just for good measure, she threw in the lasso rope. She made sandwiches and put them and a box of matches in her coat pockets. She was glad the horses were gone. What about Spike? She put food in the barn for him and propped one of the doors partly open. She returned to the kitchen and looked around.

"No telling when I'll be back," she said to herself. "The fires will go out, the food will freeze, the canned goods will burst . . . I can't help it, I see no other way—God give me strength. If I can get the car through the snow to the depot, the rest will be easy. Come along, Delores, let's go."

"I look like a stuffed-up mummy," said Delores, smiling.

Miss Martin helped her down the back steps and into the car. The engine started, and after a short delay, the car began to move.

"It'll be rough going," Miss Martin said. "Just close your eyes and relax, and then you can bear the pain better."

She drove in a zigzag path across the prairie, hunting for bare spots where the snow had blown thin. Coming to drifts, she had to get out and shovel, spread ashes in front of the wheels to get traction in the snow, then start again, crawling inch by inch. The elevator and little Oak Leaf depot seemed to move farther away with each turn of the car's wheels. Once the ashes ran out, and Miss Martin had to walk back to the school with the two buckets, go down in the cellar and get more. The second half of the journey

was easier, because the drifts were not so high. Finally the car
stalled, but within walking distance of the depot. Miss Martin
shoveled a path in the snow and helped Delores to her feet.

Inside the waiting room, Delores sat down on a low bench and
leaned against the wall. "Jeepers!" she said. "I never thought I'd
make it!"

Miss Martin gathered up kindling from the floor and soon had
a fire started in the little stove. She carried coal in the buckets from
the box in her car. Soon the little room was filled with welcome
warmth.

"I'm tired, Miss Martin." The girl's face looked so white, it
frightened her teacher.

"Lie down on these blankets on the floor," said Miss Martin.
"I'll cover you up with Grandmother's homespun and keep you
warm. Maybe the Goose will come soon—I'll flag it when it does.

The engineer knows me, he's taken me so often. Once when I was late, he backed the train up to take me on. It was Thanksgiving time, and he said he didn't want to leave me all alone in that lonesome schoolhouse over the holiday. You rest now, while I try to telephone."

"Do you know how?" asked Delores.

"Yes," said Miss Martin, "if I can get a connection. But maybe the wires are down." She pulled an electric switch on the side wall, then began turning the handle at the side. "One long and two short. John Markus, the dispatcher in town, told me to telephone the Selfridge dispatcher any time I wanted to be picked up.

Miss Martin rang and rang, but could get no response. Once a sputtering sound came over the wires, so she knew they were not entirely dead. When she saw that Delores had gone to sleep, she sat down quietly on the block of wood near the stove and rested. She was very tired. She knew she must gather all her strength together for the rest of the journey. She took the sandwiches from her pocket and ate them.

What if the Goose never came? They could stay only till their supply of coal ran out. Then, somehow, they would have to get back to the schoolhouse again. Perhaps someone would come before that. They would come to the school, find the fires out, see her car gone, follow its tracks and come to the depot. She would have to have help getting back. Who would it be?

But all this was borrowing trouble. The Goose just must come back. She had no idea what time it was. She had no watch and had left her two alarm clocks at the school. She could not remember winding them, so they had probably stopped. What did it matter? What was one hour more or less, when a child lay sick to death?

She never knew how many hours they waited, but she put the last piece of coal on the fire with a sense of resignation. All the events of the past week were jumbled together in her mind now—she could not remember what had happened or when. She could not fight the elements any more. Whatever came would have to come . . .

Meanwhile on Friday at home, Mama Wagner was beside herself with worry. Johannes came in Thursday night at midnight, bringing Darrell. He ate a hearty meal, slept for a few hours, and before daybreak started out again.

"Oh, why didn't he bring Delores home?" cried Mama.

"He couldn't," explained Darrell. "We hunted for the cattle for three hours and couldn't find them. We tried to open the road from Arlo Beckler's place over here, but we ran the tractor and snowplow in the ditch and had to leave them there. Lucky we didn't have to hunt Queen—she was out by the barn."

"Why didn't he bring Delores home?" repeated Mama.

"It was blizzarding every minute we were out," said the boy. "It felt like hail hitting you in the face—like a hundred bees biting you. Delores had a cold, she was coughing bad. You want her to be out in that, riding all around on the tractor in the wind?"

"No," said Mama. "He could have brought her straight home and then gone out again. A child should come first—before horses and cattle."

"Oh, shoot!" cried Darrell. "She's O. K. at school. Miss Martin's got coal now and it's warm. She'll take good care of her."

"Miss Martin's got plenty to do," said Mama. "Shovel coal day and night, shovel snow paths, shovel up snow-water to drink and wash in, look after a furnace and two stoves, cook meals, teach school . . . and look after a sick girl. Why can't Pop go after her?"

"He will when he finds the cattle," said Darrell. "What I'm worried about is our horses. Pop and I turned Sugar and Nellie loose before we left school last night, but they haven't come home yet. They're not used to rustling for themselves. They've had no food all week . . ."

"Horses!" cried Mama. "Horses and cattle! That's all you guys think about."

Darrell gave his mother a sharp look. Then he said, "I better go and do the chores. Got to open the tank so the stock can drink when they come. Got to keep the paths open if I can."

"The water pails are empty," said Mama. "Feed the chickens and bring in the eggs." She looked out the window. "Is that Sugar and Nellie back? I see something jumping around."

Darrell rushed out, saw the horses in the distance, but could not get to them. The wind was blowing a gale, and it took a long time to shovel to the barn. He set the buckets by the windmill and went to the old haystack by the cow-shed. He had to shovel the snow off and there was only a little hay left. The wind blew and scattered it. He took what he could into the barn for the milk-cows and saddle-horses. The two-year-olds and Patty and Queen were there now.

"I must get some oats," Darrell said to himself.

A mountainous drift had piled up between barn and granary. The wind blew fresh snow into his face as he climbed up to go over it. Before he knew he was at the top, he went tumbling down the other side and landed at the bottom, covered with snow. He shook the snow off, then went in and filled his buckets with oats.

"Oh, this mean old snow!" he cried in disgust. "I could kick it ten miles. Coming back over the drift, he held his arms outspread to keep from spilling the oats. Often he sank to his knees, but got quickly up again. He decided to dig a tunnel through it as soon as he could. He gave the oats to the cows and horses, but held some back for Sugar and Nellie.

When he came to the windmill to get the water, he discovered that it was broken. Always in the worst weather, the mill broke. Some part needed repairing or replacing. Somebody would have to go to town before it would pump water again. Darrell shoveled clean snow into his two buckets, took them in and set them on the stove.

"I froze my face," he said. "Didn't think it was that cold." He took a handful of snow from the pail and began to rub his cheek.

"Don't do that!" called Mama sharply. "Don't rub it, bathe it gently, and stay away from the stove. Remember what we read in the First Aid book? Is that snow you got there? Where's the water?"

"Windmill's broke," said Darrell gruffly. "Gotta melt snow-water."

"Well, of all things!" cried Mama. "A blizzard wouldn't be complete without the windmill breaking down."

Christy was over his cold now and feeling lively again. He pulled a chair over to the stove, climbed up and reached in the pail. "I'll hit you," he said. He made a snowball in his hands and threw it at Darrell. He was having fun.

Darrell laughed. "You hit me and I'll hit you back, boy."

"Did you bring in the eggs?" asked Mama.

"No," said Darrell. "I'm going out again to take this water to the horses."

It was a long time before he came back. When he did, his clothes were frozen stiff, but he had a bucket half full of eggs. "The wind blew the water all over me," he said. " Here's the eggs and not one broke. It's a wonder they're not all scrambled. Path's blown shut already."

"Take those wet overalls off quick," said Mama. "Put on dry ones."

"I'll get more snow first." In a few minutes he was back with two snow-filled buckets, which Mama set on the stove. He went into the side bedroom to change.

"I'm as bad as Miss Martin," said Mama, "melting snow to drink."

"Be thankful we got snow," said Darrell, with a laugh.

"No danger runnin' out of that," said Mama. "Watch Christy while I go upstairs to make the beds."

It was Christy's idea to hit Darrell with another snowball. Carefully he climbed up on the chair again, and reached deep down in the bucket for a handful of snow. But the snow had melted to water, and the water had started to boil. Quickly he snatched his hand out of the boiling water, but knocked against the side of the bucket and overturned it. The scalding water poured over his right leg above the knee, ran down and filled up his shoe. Christy screamed at the top of his voice.

Darrell rushed in from the bedroom and the next minute, was

by his side. He pulled Christy's shoe and stocking off as quickly as possible, but around his ankle, the skin and some flesh came off.

"Mama, Mama, come quick!" cried Darrell in despair.

Mama had heard the boy's cries. She came running down the stairs and into the kitchen. "Ach! What's happened now?"

Darrell pointed to Christy's leg and foot. "He got scalded. His hand's burned bad, too."

"Get the sterilized cotton and roll of bandage quick," said Mama. "Get the carbolic acid . . ."

Darrell ran to the kitchen cupboard and brought the things. Mama put a teaspoonful of the acid in a pan of water, washed the burns and wrapped them up carefully. Then she took Christy in her arms and rocked him, but he would not stop crying. His cries told her that he was in deep pain.

"We've got to take him to a doctor," said Mama. "I don't know if I did what was right."

"How can we get there?" Darrell's face was white with anxiety.

"If only your Papa would come," moaned Mama. "All day he stays out there, all day the men stand around out there, trying to dig a machine out of the snow in a ditch. Why can't they be here when we need them?"

"What you want?" demanded Darrell. "Can I carry Christy to town then? Can we walk?"

Mama gave the boy a look of scorn. Darrell couldn't stand it to hear Mama's complaining. He rushed out the door. He had to keep busy. He had to do something. He ran to the barn, floundering through the snow. He got down on his hands and knees and began to dig a tunnel through the big snowbank. The action warmed him and he felt better.

"Why don't I put out a distress signal?" he asked himself. "Maybe a plane will fly over and land. Maybe Paul Kruger will see it and come. He'll pick up Mom and Christy and take them to the doctor in town."

He brought up one load of ashes from the cellar after another. Then out in the levelest place on the prairie, to the east of the barnyard, he tramped a large plus sign on the snow and filled it with ashes. All the time he was working, the wind kept blowing snow and ashes in his face. He knew the signal would be covered up before he got back to the house, but he kept on making it just the same. It was all he could do to help get Christy to the doctor.

After a while, the signal was done and he went in.

The sight of Mama's tear-stained face bent over the sobbing Christy wrenched the boy's heart. There she sat beside the kitchen stove, rocking and rocking, forever rocking.

The boy stamped past them into the front room. He took off

his wraps and threw his overshoes across the room. He turned on the radio, but the battery was dead. He picked up a Western magazine, but could not read. He stretched out on the davenport and tried to rest, but his nerves would not let him. He knew he was listening for the roar of an airplane which never came.

"Oh, heck!" he cried in disgust. "If I'd only gone out with Pop, this would never have happened. I'll go and find the men, wherever they are."

He put his things back on and rushed out through the kitchen. But Mama stopped him. "Where are you going?" she demanded.

"Out," he said.

"Our cattle are dead and buried in the snow," said Mama, "but our horses are still jumping around. Did you catch Sugar and Nellie yet?"

"No," said Darrell. "I'm going out to hunt for them."

"Oh no you're not," said Mama. "Let the men find their old horses and cattle. You stay here. Don't you dare go out and leave me alone."

Darrell stood by the door, looking at his mother uncertainly. Then he heard the sound of a roaring motor, and before she could say another word, he was out and gone.

CHAPTER XII

After the Storm

It was not an airplane, after all.

It was Uncle Rudolph in his jeep, and that was almost as good. Darrell met him and brought him into the house.

"Where's Johannes?" asked Mama. "How many days does it take to dig a tractor out of a ditch?"

"It's out," said Rudolph. "They left the snowplow there by the road. No use plowing roads when they drift shut right away. They're hunting for the cattle—can't find them anywhere."

"The cattle?" Darrell's mouth dropped open.

"How?" asked Mama. "With the tractor?"

160

"No," said Rudolph. "On foot."

"Does Pop think . . . ?" began Darrell.

"They may be buried under the snow," said Rudolph. "They sent over for my jeep, so I could help them hunt."

"Take me to town first, Rudolph," begged Mama, "to get Christy's burns fixed. He hasn't stopped crying a minute." She told the whole story.

"O. K.," said Rudolph. "You coming too, Darrell?"

"No," said the boy. "I got to stay here and take care of the stock."

"Somebody's got to stay," said Rudolph. "No tellin' when any of us will get back."

Darrell's heart sank, as he watched the jeep leave the barnyard with Mama and Christy in it. The house was so quiet now, it was painful. Suddenly he felt hungry and got busy and fried himself some eggs. He ate them with bread and jelly and drank some left-over coffee. He looked at the kitchen clock and it was only ten in the morning. What would he do all day alone?

He went in the front room, examined the radio and took the storage battery out. He made some holes in one end with a nail, poured some vinegar in and set it on the back of the stove to soak. Maybe the vinegar would make the battery work again. After that, there was nothing to do. About two o'clock he felt hungry and fried some onions to eat with scrambled eggs. He found a box of cocoa and made cocoa to drink. After eating he fell asleep on the davenport in the front room.

When he woke up it was late afternoon and he went out to do the chores. Sugar and Nellie had not come back and that worried him. He completed the tunnel to the granary and crawled through it. He brought back grain for the chickens and fed them, and oats for the cows and horses.

Back in the house, he melted more snow, strained and cooled it for house use. He was hungry again.

"Eggs!" he said. Large kettles full of eggs sat on the counter of the cupboard. Blizzard or no blizzard, the hens kept right on laying, and Mama had no way to get rid of any eggs. "I'm sick of eggs."

He looked over the canned stuff back of the stove, but found nothing to his liking. Whistling, he went down cellar to see what he could find. He came back with a jar of canned chicken. "Boy, am I glad!" he said. The chicken made a good supper, and there was enough left for breakfast.

He decided to stay awake all night to hear if any one came in. The plight of the cattle worried him. If the men found them and brought them back, he wanted to know it right away, so he could stop worrying. He thought of Mama and Christy too, and that rough jeep ride to town. But he was comforted in the thought that they would soon reach a doctor and get Christy's burns fixed up. The wind seemed to be dying down a little . . . To his surprise, he woke up from a deep sleep and saw that morning had come.

"It's not blizzarding any more," he said thankfully. "Pop and the others will be back today sometime. What day is it? Oh yes— Saturday."

When he came in after doing the morning chores, he was surprised to find Papa and Phil sitting at the kitchen table eating fried eggs.

"Where's Mama?" asked Papa.

Darrell told about Christy's burns and the jeep ride to town.

"We thought Rudolph must have got his jeep stuck," said Papa. "Couldn't understand why he didn't come. Man alive, we're stiff from all this walking."

"The cattle—where are they?" demanded Darrell.

"Can't find 'em anywhere," said Papa. "We walked over to the stacks where they were before the blizzard, but they're not there. We walked over to Arlo's place, then to Burgard's, and down to our old dam and they're not there."

"Maybe they got drownded," said Phil. "That ice has got deep water under it."

"Don't think so," said Papa. "More likely to be buried under a big drift. They'll be alive if they don't choke from snow plugging their noses. But this soft wet snow is bad."

"Ozzie's gone over to Holzhauer's," said Phil.

"We'll go back to Burgard's again," said Papa. "I think the wind must a blown 'em over that way. We'll ride Patty and Queen to save our legs."

"Oh Pop!" cried Darrell. "Can't I go along? It's no fun stayin' here all by myself."

"You want the furnace and the kitchen fire to go out and freeze everything up?" growled Papa. "Who'd do the chores if you wasn't here?"

"Oh, shoot!" cried Darrell in disgust.

Papa and Philip rode the horses out of the barnyard and were gone.

About two that afternoon, Darrell went upstairs and looked out the windows on all sides. To the south he saw two small specks.

"The horses!" he cried. "That's Sugar and Nellie. I'll go get them and ride south and look for the cattle. Maybe I'll find 'em before Pop does. Then won't he be surprised!"

He put on his wraps, found a rope and started walking south across the snow-covered prairie. It was not snowing and there was no wind, but it was bitter cold. He knew it must be below zero. Rover came part way with him, and he chased him back. In some places, the snow was as high as the fence posts, in others, it had drifted in ridges ten or fifteen feet high. It was hard walking and he had to stop often to rest. He saw the two horses ahead, not far away.

He walked more slowly now. When he got to the horses, they acted frightened, ready to turn and run. He came up quietly, talking in a low voice. Now they knew him, but were still afraid. They tried to walk away, but a high snowbank blocked them. He walked up to Sugar and caught her. He threw himself up on her back and chased Nellie over to the railroad track, where there wasn't so much snow. He chased her up the track till he got close to home. Then he rode ahead on Sugar, and Nellie followed.

He put the horses in the barn and fed them oats. He felt happy to have them back. "Sugar and Nellie," he said, "you're awfully thin. That comes from riding you to school and having nothing to eat up there."

The horses whinnied eagerly. Darrell patted their noses as they ate. He talked to them as if they were people. Then a sudden thought struck him—how would Delores get home from school without a horse to ride? But he pushed the thought into the back part of his mind. Delores was all right up there in the warm school, with Miss Martin looking after her. He'd go up and get her—as soon as they found the cattle.

There was no hay for Sugar and Nellie. He wished he could

get some from the haystacks out on the range, or from the hayrack, wherever it was.

"The cattle," he thought. "I must help find them." A terrible thought struck him, that after the long search, they would find the cattle dead. Mom was always pessimistic, but maybe she knew. "If Pop loses them all, we will lose three thousand dollars—and that's no chicken-feed money."

"I've got to find the cattle," said Darrell to himself. "Which way shall I go? No use going where the men have been . . ." Suddenly, the thought of Delores came to him—Delores sick at school. Maybe the cattle were up by the elevator. They often came there. He'd go up and see. He'd ride Nellie instead of Sugar. Nellie was stronger and could bring them both back through the deep snow. He could bring Delores home, anyhow.

Definite purpose gave him courage. Nellie moved along steadily, and by following the railroad, it did not take too long. The boy's distant sight was good. He had "the far look in his eyes," like all West River boys. Long before he reached the elevator, he saw that no cattle were there. So he took a diagonal shortcut across to the schoolhouse.

Looking ahead, he was surprised to see no smoke coming out of the chimney. He knew Miss Martin had plenty of coal now. Could something have happened? Snow covered the open front porch—it had not been swept that morning, nor the front door opened.

"They're just lazy," he said to himself. "They've been living in the two rooms at the back. They've let the furnace fire go out— they're too lazy to shovel coal." But even as he said the words, fear clutched at his heart.

He rode quickly around to the teacherage door and tied Nellie to the railing. Miss Martin never locked any doors. He ran up the snow-covered steps and without stopping to knock, opened the door. The fire was out, the room was cold. It was so cold that even with his sheepskin on, he shivered. "They're not here!" he said aloud.

One step, a glance in the bedroom and the unmade bed, and he knew that something had happened. Where were they? Where had they gone? He put his hand to his head and tried to think. To one of the neighbors, of course. Which house was the nearest— the Sticklemeyers or the Hummels? Where had they gone and why? Delores was sick when he last saw her. Her cold must have grown worse. Miss Martin must have taken her . . .

The car! Why hadn't he thought of it before? He rushed out. The car . . . it was gone. They'd gone off in the car. Which direction? When? How long ago? It stormed all day Thursday and half of Friday, and the wind had never stopped blowing since then. If they went before the storm was over, there would be no trace of their tracks in the snow.

He ran out to see. He could make out faint tracks running from the teacherage door toward the deserted house. Had they gone there, or on out to the Hummels? Then he looked over toward the elevator and saw the car. It was stalled in a low place, half-hidden by the depot, and the snow had drifted, almost covering it. He jumped on Nellie's back and rode over. He got off the horse and walked all around the car. It would take a tractor to pull it out.

Where had they gone from here? To the Hummels? That was three miles further on, and the worst road around. It would have

meant hard walking. On the train? But no trains had been running for days . . . He ran to the depot and looked in. The waiting
room looked just the same as it had always looked. There was
not a single clue that a woman and a girl had spent agonizing
hours there such a short time before.

Darrell came out, jumped on Nellie's back and scanned the
horizon. Once he thought he heard a strange moaning sound.
Was it the wind? It couldn't be a person, could it? Somebody
in pain or trouble? The cattle—did it sound like cows? He looked
all around but saw not a living thing. He stopped to look under
the loading chute of the stock-pen, where he had found the Indian
woman. Then he came back to Miss Martin's car. He could not
understand it. Quickly he rode back to the schoolhouse. Maybe
they had left a note.

He tied Nellie up and went in again. He hunted carefully, but
found no note. There was nothing to indicate where the two

might have gone. The rooms were cold and empty.

"I'll build up the fire in the furnace," Darrell said aloud. "That will keep the building warm and keep Miss Martin's food from freezing. Then I'll go first to one neighbor's, then to the other's." He had to wait a long time to get the fire started, to check it before leaving.

When he came up from the cellar, his task completed, he went into the little bedroom. He looked out toward the elevator, to assure himself that Miss Martin's car was still there. But he never saw the car at all.

"Cattle!" he gasped. A bunch of cattle were scattered around the elevator. "Where did they come from? They might be ours!"

He tore out of the building at top speed. In his anxiety over Delores and Miss Martin, he had almost forgotten the cattle. And there they were, right under his nose. He could have kicked himself for not finding them so near at hand. They must have been huddled in the corner against the elevator on the far side, to keep out of the wind. Dunderhead—why didn't he have sense enough to go look on the other side? That sound he heard must have been their bawling—faint because they were weak from cold and hunger.

He rode over and looked at them, and the sight made him feel sick. They were caked in snow and ice, body, head and eyes. Soft snow had frozen in their hair so hard and stiff they could hardly walk. They were Pop's cattle all right. He was sure of that. The wind had changed and they had come out to look for grass. How could they rustle grass when they could hardly stand up?

But they were still alive. At least, some of them were. What luck for Pop!

Darrell stared at the cows and tried to think. He felt first relief to have found them, and found them safe, then anxiety—how could he get them home? He would need help to get them home alive. Pop and Ozzie and Phil would all have to help. The cows were so weak, they might have to be carried home in a truck. He'd have to ride home first and find the men—no telling where they were, off on the prairies each in a different place, searching. Would the cattle stay where they were, or drift with the wind and get buried in snow?

He could only hope. The thing to do now was to get home as quickly as he could. He slapped Nellie sharply and started off. Going south along the tracks, he heard what he thought was the sound of a motor. Could it be Uncle Rudolph had come back with the jeep and was bringing the men? He turned and faced the other way. He wanted to be sure the cattle were still there. He wanted to be sure it was not all a dream that he had found them. He could see them, more scattered out now, staggering from hunger and weakness. Some had fallen down. Golly! If he didn't hurry, they'd all be dead soon.

Then above, he saw an airplane flying and he heard the roaring of its motor. He stared. Was it Paul Kruger? No, it was a much larger plane. Perhaps some pilot had seen his signal, after all, and had come to help. The plane was flying very low. Was it in trouble, trying to make a forced landing? Or, was it coming down to pick someone up? The thought of Delores and Miss Martin hit him so hard, his heart started pounding. Maybe he'd missed them the way he'd missed the cattle. He felt like kicking himself. Dunderhead! Why couldn't he find them, if they were around somewhere, near?

He watched the plane. Whoever he was, the pilot was flying too low. He was flying over the elevator now.

"Criminy sakes! He hit it! Something fell off the top!" shouted Darrell. "He's taking the roof off the elevator, the crazy fool! He's going in circles! Hey, you!" Darrell waved his arm and shouted. "What the heck are you doing? Stunt-flying?"

Then he saw objects falling one after the other—big, heavy, dark objects falling to the ground. The pilot had not hit the elevator at all. He was not trying to land. He was flying over the herd of cattle and dropping bales of hay for them to eat.

"Well, I'll be jiggered! It's the haylift!" Darrell had heard about it over the radio. Now he was seeing it with his own eyes. "He's dropping baled hay! Hay for our cattle to eat!"

He waved and waved his cap in the air, and shouted as loud as he could, while Nellie danced around. He wished the pilot would see him and come over and land, so he could thank him. Gratitude

engulfed him as never before in all his young life. But the plane circled the elevator once more and then disappeared in the sky, flying south.

"Let's go home, Nellie." Darrell took a deep breath. "The cattle will stay there now, all right. Won't Pop and Phil and Ozzie be surprised!"

But all the way home his heart was heavy. "Where are Delores and Miss Martin? Why couldn't I find them too?"

When he rode into the barnyard, he saw Patty and Queen tied to the fence-posts and knew the men had come back. He left Nellie at the barn and ran in, bursting with eagerness to tell his story, but he had no chance.

Uncle Rudolph was standing there by the kitchen stove, talking in a low voice. He must have just come. No jeep was outside— how did he get there? Had he walked? Something was wrong. Darrell could tell by the serious look on the men's faces.

"Christy's burns?" he blurted out. "Did Mom do something wrong?"

Uncle Rudolph turned and looked at Darrell. "The burns are bad, but they will heal all right—in time. It's Delores we're worried about."

"Delores?" gasped Darrell. "She's not at school and Miss Mar-

tin's not there either. I went there to bring Delores home. Where
did they go?"

"Delores is in the hospital in town," said Uncle Rudolph. "She
was operated on for appendicitis this morning. The appendix had
burst twenty-four hours before."

Papa Johannes just sat there, his hand covering up his face.

"Is she . . . bad?" asked Phil. "Is she going to die?"

"How did she ever get to town?" demanded Darrell.

"She's still on the danger list," said Uncle Rudolph, "a very
sick girl."

"But how did she ever . . ." Darrell could not finish his question.

"Miss Martin took her to Oak Leaf depot in her car and waited
there I don't know how many hours," said Uncle Rudolph, "until
the Galloping Goose finally came. It got stalled a dozen times,
another snowplow banged into it and wrecked the end of the
caboose where they were riding. The train men got word to the
dispatcher. The doctor rode out on the tracks in his car and brought
them in—that last mile, after midnight, last night. They operated
this morning. Miss Martin stayed with her through it all."

Papa Johannes took out his handkerchief and mopped his fore-
head. "Here I thought *we* was havin' things hard."

"Where's Mom?" asked Darrell. "Does she know?"

"It took us most of the day yesterday to get to town," said Uncle
Rudolph. "Even the jeep can't take drifts over four feet high, so
I had to stop and shovel a hundred times. Christy screamed the
whole day, but we got there . . . late, about dark. The doctor at
the hospital fixed Christy's burns up and told Minna to bring him
back this morning, so he could dress the burns again. She was just

going *in* the hospital, when she met Miss Martin coming *out.*"

"Before, or after?" asked Papa.

"The operation was over," said Uncle Rudolph. "The doctor said Delores is holding her own. Minna's going to stay in town. Lavina hasn't room for her. She and Miss Martin will be sleeping at Gustaf's. You boys will have to do your own cooking."

No one smiled. Cooking seemed, just then, a little thing to do.

"Where's Christy?" asked Darrell. "He staying too?"

"Oh, I forgot." Uncle Rudolph laughed. "Where's your tractor, Johannes?"

"Out by the barn," said Papa. "I finally got it back."

"Come and pull me out of the ditch then," said Rudolph.

"But where's Christy?" cried Darrell. "Is Mom keeping him in town?"

"No," laughed Uncle Rudolph. "He wouldn't stay, the little wretch. Not at Lavina's nor Grandma Wagner's nor at Gustaf's. He yelled and fussed. He wanted a jeep-ride home, so I brought him."

"Where is he?" asked Phil.

"In the jeep, in the ditch," laughed Uncle Rudolph. "Asleep— at least, I hope he's still asleep, all wrapped up in blankets. About three miles east. I left the jeep there and walked over."

"He might wake up and drive it off," laughed Oscar. "Remember that time he turned on the ignition and the tractor started going, and scared his poor Mom half to death?"

"Yes," grinned Darrell. "I jumped on, pulled the switch and stopped it. That's once Christy got a licking."

"Criminy sakes!" cried Johannes. "You go, Phil, get the tractor quick. Hurry, before he wakes up and yells his head off. Ozzie and I will start out again up north, lookin' for those pesky cattle."

"The CATTLE!" shouted Darrell. "Jeepers! I'd forgotten all about them for once. Why, I . . . I FOUND THE CATTLE!"

"You sure?" demanded Papa. "Where?"

"Why didn't you say so?" asked Phil.

"How come?" cried Oscar.

"This was one time I thought of Delores and Christy first," said Darrell. Then he told the whole story of the empty schoolhouse and the haylift by the elevator.

"Well, I'll be jiggered!" shouted Phil.

"Let them eat hay!" cried Papa Johannes.

"I'll sleep tonight," said Ozzie, "for the first time since this blizzard began. How many weeks has it been blizzarding, anyhow?"

CHAPTER XIII

Digging Out

Christy was not harmed by his three-hour nap in the stalled jeep, but as soon as he got home, he cried for his mother. Every day Darrell had to explain that Mama was in town and would be back soon. Every day Darrell had to dress the boy's burns, using medications sent out by the doctor. Soon Christy was running about as usual.

The big boys missed their mother too, especially at mealtime.

"Hope she'll bring some groceries," said Darrell, "so we can have something decent to eat." He turned the burned potatoes in the skillet.

"How about pigs-in-blankets and sour cream *knipfla?*" asked Philip. "Will that do?"

"I want *kuga,* I want *kuga!*" cried Christy.

"And sour cream custard *kuga* and pickled watermelon and ripe olives," Phil went on.

"When do we get it?" demanded Darrell.

"Not till the blizzard's over," said Phil complacently. "The roads are plugged now for good. It'll take an airplane to get Mama home."

"Which blizzard? The next one or the last one?" asked Darrell.

"There's always a new one blowing in while the last one's blowing out," said Phil.

"I don't mind the blizzarding so much," said Darrell. "It's exciting while it lasts. What gets me is what comes after—this eternal waiting, when the roads stay plugged for weeks, when the storm keeps slapping back at you, when the coal gets low and the groceries run out . . . no telephone, no newspaper, a dead radio. Cut off from the whole world, penned up in the house . . ."

"You can go out whenever you want to," said Oscar.

"Yes, go out and shovel the paths open," said Darrell, "then wait while the wind blows them shut again."

After a dinner of burned fried potatoes, the boys lounged on the davenport, while Oscar tinkered with the battery of the radio. In late afternoon, Darrell looked out the west window at the setting sun.

"Look at the sundogs," he said. "They look like fingers sticking up, and they're colored like a rainbow."

"I think this battery's got a little life in it yet," said Oscar.

"I put vinegar in it. Maybe that helped." Darrell grinned, as

Christy climbed on his lap and started to box with him.

Oscar replaced the battery, the radio began to sputter and soon a voice could be dimly heard. The boys bent their heads close to listen. Darrell had to hold his hand over Christy's mouth so they could hear. The announcement was very faint, then it faded out again.

"Well, I'll be jiggered!" cried Phil. "U. S. Army bulldozers coming!"

"Five big caterpillar bulldozers starting out in this territory!" cried Phil.

"That's once President Truman remembered us," laughed Oscar.

The three boys looked at each other in silence. Suddenly they were startled by a loud crash. It sounded like the smashing of a cupboard full of dishes. Broken glass flew in every direction, as the boys jumped wide-eyed to their feet. Christy began to shriek at the top of his voice.

"Criminy sakes!" shouted Darrell. "What was that?" He grabbed Christy in his arms and held him close.

"Somebody got a gun?" gasped Phil.

"Look there!" said Oscar. "Look what we got."

Their eyes went from the jagged hole in the east window to the floor. There, surrounded by pieces of broken window pane, lay a beautiful Chinese Ringneck cock pheasant, killed by the blow.

"He must a been flyin' into the setting sun," said Oscar, and got blinded. Couldn't see where he was goin' and hit the window." He picked the bird up. "Not so skinny either. He's been feedin' in somebody's chicken coop."

The boys looked at each other and grinned.

"A nice change from eggs," said Darrell. "I'll get the frying pan. Clean up the broken glass, Phil."

"I'll get some boards and block up the broken window," said Oscar.

"To get a pheasant as easy as that," laughed Phil. "I went hunting three times last fall and didn't get a single one."

Oscar dressed and cooked the pheasant like chicken. When Johannes came in, they had a feast. All through the meal, they talked about the big bulldozers and caterpillar tractors, and wondered when they would come.

"Those cats are not allowed to go over bridges," said Philip, "they're so heavy. They've got to go around. Sometimes they slide into a creek full of snow nose first. Then they have to bring another cat to pull it out."

"They're slow," said Oscar. "They can barely travel three miles an hour. They'll get here by grasshopper time next summer."

"Guess we won't wait for no U. S. Army bulldozer," said Johannes. "When we're sure it's stopped snowing, we'll plow out our own roads."

Not till several nights later did the unexpected happen. The thunderous roar of a motor woke Darrell and the men from a heavy sleep. Quickly they threw on their clothes and outer wraps and hurried out. There by the kitchen doorstep sat the most welcome sight they had ever seen—a huge caterpillar tractor with a bulldozer blade in front for pushing the snow.

"Build up the fire, Darrell," shouted Papa, "and put plenty coffee on."

Beside the huge machine stood Al Sticklemeyer, grinning from ear to ear. The men driving were strangers.

"We've come to let you out!" shouted Al, above the roar of

the motor. "I came along to show the U. S. Army the way. Been workin' day and night—all the roads blocked, but they won't be for long." The huge machine crawled slowly across the barn-yard, pushing a mountain of snow before it.

"Criminy!" cried Darrell, standing in the doorway. "Now at last we can get *out*!"

But the machine had stalled, for the roar of the motor had died down. Darrell ran out to see what the trouble was. The men were all gathered round the highest drift on the far side of the cowshed. They were all shoveling. What was the trouble? Darrell came closer and looked. The bright lights on the caterpillar showed the forms of three cows in the snowbank, sealed up by snow and ice. He turned away. He could not bear to look at it. Right back of the barn too.

After a while the men came in, talking and laughing. Darrell fried eggs for them and they all drank coffee. But they did not

stay long. Other farmers were waiting to be dug out. The huge "cat" went lumbering off, and the roar of its motor faded away, leaving the Wagner farmhouse to its former silence.

The next morning Darrell heard a familiar whistle. "The Galloping Goose!" he cried. "The Goose has come back. They're opening up the branch line." He took Christy to the window to look.

Across the snow on the railroad tracks, they saw a long train puffing slowly along. Three steam locomotives were hooked up in a snow unit special, which included the snowplow and a cut widener and a crew of thirty shovelers. Behind the snow equipment was a doubleheader with eighteen cars of coal and oil, and three cars of merchandise, groceries and cattle feed.

"See the big train," said Christy. "See the engine throw the snow out."

"People up in North Dakota must be scraping the bottom of the barrel, just like us," said Darrell.

"Who wants to go to town?" shouted Uncle Rudolph, appearing in his jeep.

No one needed a second invitation. With little Christy, the two boys and three men bent double and crowded in. Although the caterpillar had opened the prairie road and the Yellowstone trail, going was rough. The wind had blown snow over the road in many places and the deep ruts had frozen hard. The jeep rocked up and down and back and forth, but finally reached town.

"Man alive!" exclaimed Darrell, stepping out in front of Jen's Café. "Looks like they had a little snow here too."

A narrow pathway was opened up between mountainous piles of snow, which blocked the light from the store show windows.

Only a few cars were out. Others were still buried under great piles of snow. The snow seemed to silence all sounds.

"Jeepers creepers!" whispered Phil. "It's like a cemetery. Where are all the people?"

"In bed, hibernating like bears," said Oscar. "They got sense."

Johannes Wagner, carrying Christy in his arms, tried the door of the café, but found it locked. "Looks like we go hungry," he said. "No stores open. This ain't Sunday, is it?"

"Barber shop closed too," said Oscar. "And boy, do I need a haircut!"

Only postoffice and drugstore were open. Darrell ran in and bought several packages of salted sunflower seeds. "Where do we go now?"

"To the hospital," said Papa Johannes.

The nurse looked at the row of five men and one three-year-old who wanted to visit her patient, severely. "Five minutes," she said.

Delores was alone, sitting up in bed for the first time. She looked thin and pale, but had a broad smile on her face.

"Pretty little blizzard, that snowstorm of yours!" laughed Darrell.

"Man alive!" cried Delores. "Did we ever have the snow!"

"Snow! Ach, that was nothing!" laughed Papa.

"Here's some Rooshian peanuts," said Darrell. "Next time you and Miss Martin run off like that, please leave a note to tell where you've gone."

Delores grinned. "I thought you liked mysteries. Jeepers! What a train ride we had. I'll never forget it as long as I live. How's Sugar? Did she ever get home?"

"Yes," said Darrell, "but she looks like an old crowbait, ready to kick the bucket. All her ribs are showing. Poor old girl—nothing to eat for a whole week but Rolled Oats and a Christmas tree!"

"There's Mama!" screamed Christy. *"Mama! Mama!"*

Who should come in but Mama Wagner and Miss Martin. Christy ran to his mother, who took him up in her arms and smothered him with kisses. Then he sat on the boys' laps and started boxing with them. There was so much to tell, everybody talked at once, until the nurse came in and demanded quiet.

"I must get back to Oak Leaf School today," said Miss Martin.

"Wish I could take you," said Papa Wagner, "but the jeep's pretty crowded. Rudolph will have to make two trips as it is, to get Mama and Christy back home."

"Can't they go with me," asked Miss Martin, "in Paul Kruger's airplane? He offered to fly me out, to save time."

"Me?" cried Mama. "In an *airplane?* Ach, what next?"

It took a lot of coaxing, but in the end it seemed the best way.

The men decided to stay till evening, so they and the boys could go to the afternoon show.

"Come, Darrell," said Papa. "We go over now to see Grandma."

Grandma met them at the back door. She kissed Darrell and fell into Johannes' arms. "Ach, what a winter! Ach, what a snow-storm!" she cried. "Never even in the old country have I seen the like. That poor little girl . . ."

"She's O. K. now, Grandma," said Darrell. "She's as good as new."

"What a trip for her to make," sobbed Grandma. "And poor Grandpa . . ."

"Grandpa?" inquired Johannes. "Has something happened to him?"

"Sh!" said Grandma. "Speak softly so he will not hear. Grandpa iss in bed. He iss wore out, and he wants nobody to know. I tell only you two . . . Every day he take a walk. It was nothing to walk down to the grocery store to get a bag of groceries. That day, when the storm was bad, I said, 'No, you stay here,' but he was stubborn. He said, 'I will go. I must every day take a walk.' The storm caught him when he was halfway home. He could not see. He stumbled around, bumping into telephone poles and stalled cars. All the houses and stores was gone . . ."

"Gone?" exclaimed Darrell, open-mouthed.

"He could not find them," said Grandma. "Maybe he was in middle of street. He got so scared, he started lighting matches to see his way, to try to get warm. They kept going out. Finally, there was no more matches . . . Ach! Ach! It was terrible . . ." In her eyes was the sad expression seen in the faces of so many old-country women.

"What then?" asked Johannes. "How did he get home?"

"He fell on his hands and knees in the snow and called for help," Grandma went on. "For a long time no one came. Then Eddie Schweitzer, the garage man, found him. He brought him home half-frozen. He lost all the groceries and never found them. Our electric lights was out for two days and I had nothing to cook and a cold stove . . ."

"Is Grandpa O. K. now?" asked Johannes.

"His face, his hands and feet got frostbitten," said Grandma, "but it iss better now. The doctor says just rest he needs. To think, right here in *town* it happened! If Eddie had not come along . . . ach! ach!"

Darrell thought of the cows frozen in the snowbank, then pushed the horrible thought away. Grandpa was all right again.

"Such troubles! That little Delores and her teacher . . ."

"She's O. K. now," said Johannes. "Next week we take her home."

"I make a bouquet of beautiful chenille flowers for her," said Grandma, smiling. "I give it to her to take home."

It was a happy day for all when Delores came home from the hospital, all wrapped up in blankets, sitting beside Papa in the cab of the truck.

"Don't you fool yourself that the winter's over," teased Darrell. "*Your* blizzard was only the warming-up storm. There are dozens of others waiting to strike. All through March and April, and even into May, they can come."

"Green-up time can't come too soon for me this year," sighed Mama. "This is an awful winter, but we have to take the bad with the good."

"You *liked* your airplane ride, didn't you, Mom?" teased Darrell.

"It rode like a rocking chair," laughed Mama. "It didn't jolt like that old jeep. And it never broke down once!"

"Like a butterfly with wings, did you feel, Mama?" asked Delores.

"Ach *no!*" laughed Mama. "Don't talk so foolish. How would I look then, with wings?"

"What about all the groceries you brought, Mom?" asked Darrell. "I'm starved to death. Haven't had a decent meal since you went away."

"Tonight I cook the best supper you ever ate," said Mama.

Mama was as good as her word. She spent the whole day cooking—roast chicken, dressing, mashed potatoes and gravy, baked sweet potatoes, scalloped corn, several kinds of salad and pickles, homemade bread with butter and jelly, and sweet rice.

"Pull up your chairs," called Mama, and everybody came running.

CHAPTER XIV

Last Day of School

"Boy, it seems good to be back at school again!"

Delores put her arms around Miss Martin, who was standing on the front porch. The truck that brought her had turned around on the hill and was headed for home.

"It's good to have you strong and well again," said Miss Martin. "You'll have to take it easy for a while."

"I can't ride horseback till fall," said Delores. "I'll have to study hard to make up what I missed."

"So will all the other children," said Miss Martin. "So many snowstorms and so many absences . . . My reports look terrible."

186

Konrad Snider rode up on his horse and the Sticklemeyer children soon arrived in their cart. Then Pete Hummel drove up in his jeep, and out tumbled Peter and Hulda. Emil came riding up too, and Darrell appeared on Nellie.

"Everybody's here but Ruby," said Miss Martin. "If she comes, we'll have perfect attendance."

Winter was only a memory now, but the children still talked about the weather.

"The weather's supposed to break any day now," said Darrell. "A few weeks of thawing and we can get into the fields and plant our wheat."

"Snow's all gone except in ditches," said Jacob. "Now it's mud making all the trouble. Just look out there."

The snowbank made by the snowplow had melted and made a large mud-puddle in front of the porch, where the children had to walk.

"What we need is a dam," said Darrell. "If we banked up that water on the side of the hill, we could keep the schoolyard dry."

"And Buster could drink there!" cried Ruby Englehart. She came riding up on her new pony, with a bouquet of spring flowers in her hand. She waved good-by to her father on his white horse. He had come all the way with her.

The boys ran for shovels and set to work. They dug a large hole and piled the dirt in a bank on the lower side. The ground was so wet, the dam began to fill with water, so Peter Hummel made a spillway at one side.

"Get busy, you lazy girls!" cried Darrell.

"What can *we* do?" giggled Fernetta Sticklemeyer.

"I'm not going to do a single thing," said Ruby. "Darrell Wagner can't make me." She rode her pony to the barn and tied him up.

"We might plant trees," said Delores. "They always plant trees around a dam."

"Where you gonna find trees?" asked Konrad Snider. "There's not a tree on the whole big wide prairie."

"There is too!" shouted Delores. "There's our Christmas tree."

The Christmas tree had lasted till spring. Peter and Hulda ran to get it from its place by the teacherage door. The big snowbank was gone now, and the tree had fallen underneath. It was somewhat the worse for wear, but little Peter held it high and marched through the prairie grass with it.

"Give it to me," said Delores. "Go get the hatchet."

She chopped the side branches off with a hatchet. The little children stuck them into the banked-up pile of dirt which formed the dam. Miss Martin, wearing her sweater and high overshoes, came out to admire.

"What's this—a tree claim?" The children laughed. "In the East River country, the settlers planted trees for windbreaks."

"In the West River country too," said Emil. "But all the trees died, except a few in town."

A squawk was heard not far off and suddenly a cock pheasant flew up, a gorgeous long-tailed bird with the sun shining on the red, black and bronzy-flame color of his breast. "Oh look!" cried the children.

"So many pheasants died this winter," said Fernetta. "Pa said they came out to the trail to get something to eat and people ran over them with their cars."

"Most of 'em starved to death," said Darrell. "So much deep snow."

"Where's our Galloping Goose?" asked Peter. "Did it die too?"

"It's at my Grandma's on Oak Creek," said Ruby. "I counted seven geese when I was there, and Grandma told me to count again, because she knew she had only six. Then she counted, and found she had one extra."

"And where's Spike?" asked Peter. "We haven't seen him since the blizzards."

"Delores and I couldn't take him to town with us on our Galloping Goose ride," said Miss Martin sadly. "I left food for him. I hoped he would find his way to one of the neighbors . . ."

"We'll sure miss old Spike," said Darrell. All the children were silent, remembering.

"I saw two partridges on our way to school today," said Jacob. "One had a dark spot on his breast. They must be nesting."

"We saw some grouse," said Peter. "They've got feathers on their legs and they make a funny noise."

Miss Martin stood still and listened to the children's chatter. She was conscious of the wideness of the horizons, the blueness of the arched sky and the absolute peace which spread like a mantle over the wind-swept land. It was incredible that such a change had come in so short a time after the raging storms. Even the children's voices, telling of their close understanding and feeling for Nature, had a soothing quality. The warmth of the spring sun was making them lazy.

"I hate to call you in," said Miss Martin, "and I hate to go in myself. But we all have work to do."

"Here, Miss Martin," said Ruby, "see what I brought you." She gave her a bunch of purplish-pink pasqueflowers, which grew wild on the prairie.

"The first crocuses!" smiled Miss Martin. "Where did you find them?"

"Daddy picked them on the side of Twin Butte when he was riding herd," said Ruby.

"When the crocuses come out," laughed Jacob, "that's the time to go barefoot!"

"It's good to see crocuses again," said Miss Martin. "They are the earliest wild flowers in the prairie country. Now we know that spring is here."

They came into the schoolhouse. Miss Martin filled a glass with water and set the bouquet on her desk. The boys crowded into the front hall and took off their coats and muddy overshoes.

"Teacher says it's *spring*!" sniffed Emil. "We can't even move our tractor. It's standing hub-deep in mud."

"Boy, have we ever got the water!" cried Jacob. "The creeks are overflowing, and our dam's flooding the spillway."

"The ice in the Big Muddy's expected to go out any day now," said Konrad.

"I thought we'd be in the fields, seeding, by this time," said Darrell.

"The brown prairie grass is turning a little bit green," said Peter.

"I sure hope this sun keeps on shining, so we can get in the fields," said Jacob. "Once we start, we won't stop for anything—but rain. Nothing sweeter than the hum of half-a-dozen tractors all night long . . ."

"We got to get our wheat seeded early this year," said Darrell, "so we can make a good crop. I'm gonna hurry home tonight and fan grain. We got all the machinery to overhaul . . ."

The boys came in, and all the children took their seats.

"Jeepers creepers! It's hot in here," cried Darrell. "Miss Martin, can we open the windows?"

Miss Martin nodded and the boys opened several.

"Hear the meadow larks!" cried Delores.

The cheerful whistling sounds came in sharp and clear. The children looked up from their books to listen.

"The song of the meadow lark never sounded so sweet before," said Miss Martin.

The children smiled, remembering the long, hard winter.

"I'm sure glad summer is coming," said little Hulda.

"Yah!" scoffed Emil. "One hundred and ten every day and no trees and no shade to sit in."

"Who wants trees, anyway?" cried Delores. "They just fence you in. I like to see the whole big wide prairie and nothing else."

"And wind storms and hail storms—that's what summer brings," said Darrell. "Hope our crop don't get hailed out this year."

"Or et out by grasshoppers," added Jacob.

"Or dried up by drouth," said Emil.

"Last summer, the wind blew our chicken coops down," said Peter, "and smashed them all to pieces. It blew the feathers off all our chickens too."

The children laughed. They knew, as well as their parents, the hazards and difficulties of prairie farming.

That day after school, all the children crowded round to see Ruby get started for home on her new pony.

"Let's see you get on," said Fernetta.

"I'm tired of riding behind Daddy," bragged Ruby, "and I'm sick of bobsleds—I got dumped out so many times. I hate riding in jeeps and tractors, and that crazy old cart of the Sticklemeyers—

that's the worst of all. I'll never ride in it again."

"If I remember right, Buckskin wouldn't take you," sniffed Fernetta. "You were one too many—Buckskin didn't like you."

"Buster likes me, if Buckskin don't," said Ruby.

"Since when do you know how to ride alone?" asked Peter.

Ruby tossed her head. "I always knew. I been riding since I was a baby."

"Jeepers!" laughed Emil. "She'll be ridin' in the rodeo this fall."

Darrell tightened the cinch and Ruby got on Buster like an experienced rider. The pony began to dance a jig and Ruby began to scream.

"You go ride by her, Darrell, and get Buster started off home," called Delores, from the cab of the truck. Phil had come over to get her.

"Oh shoot!" answered Darrell. "Let Buster buck her off. That would serve Ruby right." But he rode Nellie over, took Buster's rein and led the pony as far as the railroad tracks. Then he turned him loose and rode south, while Ruby and Buster went trotting amiably off on the road going west.

Weeks rolled by, final tests came, and then it was time for the school picnic on the last day of school. Because of rain the night before, the plan for going to Oak Creek had to be given up and the picnic held in the schoolhouse. Everybody came, young and old. The women brought huge kettles filled with food—potato salad, baked beans, cheese and meat sandwiches, ripe olives, salads of various kinds, and elaborate layer cakes, trimmed with fancy frosting.

Miss Martin and the girls put the two tables together and covered them with flowered cloths. While the coffee was being made on the kerosene stove in the teacherage kitchen, the men and children waited on the front steps. Peter Hummel brought out the lasso rope, and Johannes Wagner gave a rope-jumping demonstration. The older boys, Philip Wagner and Hans and Fritz Holzhauer, jumped too, but none could jump "pepper" as fast as Johannes. He jumped until he was out of breath and had to sit down on the steps to rest.

"Come and eat!" called Mama Wagner, and everybody came, filling the benches by the tables and some of the desks. The food was good, and they all talked with their mouths full. The littlest children ran in and out, tumbled and fell, shouted and screamed. After leaving the table, they came running back, took large pieces of cake in their hands and got crumbs all over the desks and the floor. The coffee pot was soon emptied, and more put on to boil.

"Come, Miss Martin," begged Delores in the kitchen. "Come and sit down and eat. They all want to hear our story—about our ride on the Galloping Goose."

"I'll take care of the coffee," said Mama Wagner, coming out. "You go in and visit a little, Miss Martin."

"There's nothing much to tell," Miss Martin said, as they made room for her at the head of the table. "I just had to get Delores to the doctor—that's all." She told the story as simply as she could.

"I didn't know I could cause so much trouble," said Delores gently.

Just then Mama Wagner came in from the kitchen, holding her hands mysteriously behind her. Papa Wagner called out: "More coffee, please."

"Me too." Christy, sitting on his father's lap, held out his cup.

"Christy drinks *coffee*?" asked Mrs. Englehart.

Delores flushed red. "Papa did it. It's Papa's fault. Papa started him."

"I give mine coffee when they're babies," said Mrs. Sticklemeyer, "and it ain't killed one of 'em yet." Everybody laughed.

"Well, this is not coffee," Mama Wagner said. "The coffee's not on the boil yet, that old kerosene stove's so slow. But I got something else." She brought out a large bunch of red, pink and white crepe paper roses, and shyly held them out toward Miss Martin.

"We wanted . . . it was right you should have . . . something for . . . to remember . . ." Mama's words were getting all mixed up. She was not used to making speeches. She began to tremble and tears came to her eyes. "These flowers, they ain't much, I don't have time like Grandma Wagner does to make them out of that chenille stuff . . . and it costs too much money if you're not sure of a good wheat crop. We didn't know if you would like it . . .

just old paper flowers that collect the dust, but they're pretty anyhow, when they're new. I always say a woman's got to have something else to do besides work all the time . . ."

"Ach! Now, why don't you stop talking and give them to Teacher?" interrupted Johannes. "We got to get back to our seeding, me and the boys."

Mama thrust the flowers out. "It's not much for what you did for our little girl, but we give you our thanks."

Miss Martin took the bouquet, and the next minute she and Mama Wagner were locked in a close embrace. Delores put her arms around them both. Then she took the flowers from Miss Martin, put them in an empty milk bottle and set them on top of the old piano that wouldn't play any more.

"Look!" cried Delores, pointing. "Right under George Washington's picture." Everybody clapped and began to say nice things to Miss Martin.

"We hope you won't ever have such a bad winter again," said Mrs. Sticklemeyer.

"It comes only once in fifty years," laughed Pete Hummel.

"Picnic's over!" Johannes pushed back his bench and stood up. "Come on, boys. Let's get back to work. *Seeding-time is here again.*"

"Ach! What music to hear!" cried Al Sticklemeyer. "Let's all hope and pray for a good crop."

The men stalked out, while the women gathered up kettles, dishes, left-over food and children. Miss Martin tried to be everywhere at once, clearing things up, piling books in piles, and passing out report cards.

"Did I pass?" "Did I pass?" clamored the children.

"Everybody passed," said Miss Martin. She smiled as she watched the children go rushing out. She smiled, although her eyes were filled with tears. "Another school year is over," she said softly.

"Yes," said Delores, "the best year of all."

A truck out in front began to honk noisily. Papa Wagner was anxious to be off.

"Miss Martin, you coming back next year?" asked Delores quickly.

"I don't know, Delores," said Miss Martin. "The school may be closed. You may have to go to school in town. That's what you've been wanting . . ."

"Oh no," said Delores. "I like it better here, even with all the snowstorms."

"But you must grow up, Delores, and go on to better things."

The truck honked again. Darrell put his head in. "Pop's mad— waiting so long for you, Delores," he called. "We gotta get home. Come *on*."

"Miss Martin . . ."

"It's been a hard year," Miss Martin said, "but a good one, hasn't it? One we will always remember."

Delores kissed her and ran out.

A sudden gust of wind came up, and the school door blew shut behind her.

The End